"Ava, it's me, Faisal."

She hadn't heard right and yet she had. The voice, the words, even the shoes. It all came together. All of it was familiar. The fear fell away. She relaxed in his arms, her heart pounding a zillion times an hour.

"If I let you go, promise me you won't run," he said.

"It's a mistake to be here with me."

His arm eased and she slid down, landing on her feet and turning to face him.

The look he gave her was both intimidating and full of concern. "You could have died, running the way you did."

"But I didn't," she said obstinately as if her earlier fears had been based on nothing but her imagination. "It was a mistake to follow me," she repeated, for he hadn't responded the first time she'd said it. "Fai," she whispered. "You need to get out of here. Trust me."

"We'll get out of here together. It's what I do, protect."

SHEIK DEFENSE

RYSHIA KENNIE

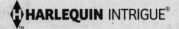

If you are reading this dedication, this one is for you. You are the reason this book was published. Thank you and enjoy.

ISBN-13: 978-1-335-72112-9

Sheik Defense

Copyright © 2017 by Patricia Detta

Recycling programs for this product may not exist in your area.

Printed in U.S.A.

www.Harlequin.com

Ryshia Kennie has received a writing award from the City of Regina, Saskatchewan, and was also a semifinalist for the Kindle Book Awards. She finds that there's never a lack of places to set an edge-of-the-seat suspense, as prairie winters find her dreaming of warmer places for heart-stopping stories. They are places where deadly villains threaten intrepid heroes and heroines who battle for their right to live or even to love. For more, visit ryshiakennie.com.

Books by Ryshia Kennie

Harlequin Intrigue

Desert Justice

Sheik's Rule
Sheik's Rescue
Son of the Sheik
Sheik Defense

Suspect Witness

CAST OF CHARACTERS

Sheik Faisal Al-Nassar—A risk taker who loves snowboarding, Faisal heads the Wyoming Branch of Nassar Security. He has more than he bargained for when the case involves a woman he once loved. Is Ava an innocent damsel in distress or part of a much deadlier scheme?

Ava Adams—She always wanted more than friendship from Faisal. Now she discovers that the man she has always loved and never forgotten is the only one who can save her.

Dan Adams—Ava's father and the Al-Nassars' family friend may be at the heart of what's going on but the knowledge he possessed disappeared when he was reported lost at sea.

Sheik Talib Al-Nassar—Faisal's older brother has his back but will he be able to help Faisal now?

Sheik Emir Al-Nassar—The head of Nassar Security provides insight as he monitors his friend's disappearance from afar.

Zafir Al-Nassar—Vice president of Nassar Security. He has his own thoughts on the plight of their family friend.

Jer Keller—A pilot and friend of Faisal who flies their rescue mission. Does his easygoing nature hide something more deadly?

Ben Whyte—Dan Adams's business partner may have been on the missing yacht. And if he was, where is he now?

Darrell Chan—This wealthy foreigner appears to have been fleeced by Dan Adams. But is that the way it all came down?

Aaron Detrick—An undercover operative with the Royal Canadian Mounted Police, he has knowledge of Darrell Chan that throws a shadow of suspicion on the tycoon.

Chapter One

Friday, June 10—11:00 p.m.

"Son of a…"

The broken expletive was followed by a bang that seemed to echo through the bowels of the yacht.

Ava Adams's eyelids fluttered. Fitfully, she turned once, then twice. The yacht shifted and rocked in the waves. It had been a late night yesterday and the day before, not to mention the fact that this trip had been completely unexpected. She was dreaming—there was no reason to get up, not yet…not for hours yet.

Still, she shivered. Her sleep was skating on the edge of consciousness—what was reality and what was not were no longer clear. In her dream, she only knew that she needed to escape. She flung one arm out grazing the wall, causing her to turn to her other side.

She opened her eyes. She wasn't fully awake. She didn't even take in her surroundings before immediately closing her eyes again. But she couldn't shift as deep into sleep as she'd been. In fact, now with her eyes closed, her consciousness was heating up. She could see through the curtain of lashes. The moonlight drifted in a faint stream of light across the sheet that twisted around her waist. Her breathing leveled out and she fell asleep again. This time the sleep was even lighter than it had been before—more troubled. She didn't know how long she slept. She only knew that it wasn't long before she was again awakened. This time by sounds that she couldn't ignore. They were loud against the background of the once calm rocking of the boat. Her senses came awake, first noting the change in smell. She inhaled, long and slow. She'd done that often in the two days that they'd been anchored in this cove. She loved the hint of vanilla that was so pervasive and wove through the salty scent of ocean, of seawater. Oddly, the vanilla scent was gone.

"To hell—" a man's voice rose in a shout. It was a shout that seemed to be cut off as if forcibly stopped. He might have said something else. Words that jumbled in the scuffle and chaos of noise that preceded a crash, followed by another.

It was only a nightmare. It was a figment of her imagination. A result of the stress of stepping from one world into another; from academia into the world of a self-sufficient adult. Two weeks from today she was moving to Casper, Wyoming. At twenty-five and with a doctorate in psychology under her belt, it was about time. At least that was what she'd told herself. Her father had encouraged her to take all the time she needed. She knew that was a way of keeping her close, of keeping her dependent on him. Even though she had lived her own life, in her own apartment, paying as many of her college bills herself as she could with money she had made by occasionally tutoring other students, still she had relied on him. It gave him a chance to be the father he hadn't gotten to be when she truly had been a child. She'd allowed him that. For he'd become her parent in her latter childhood. It had been through marriage, but stepparent or not, she couldn't ask for a better father. Now they were making up for lost time. Thus, this trip. They both needed it—the time to be together. Life had gotten busy.

She hovered in the abyss between sleeping and wakefulness. But soon sleep was completely chased away as the shouts rose in volume. More disturbing was the absolute silence that followed. That brought her to full consciousness. She was still, hardly breathing, straining to hear. Were the voices real or only her imagination, or part of a dream? Seconds ticked by. She lay tense, unmoving. The conversation she'd had with her father earlier ran uninvited through her mind. Some, if not all, of the things he had said had been disturbing. He said he was concerned that his partner had gotten himself into a situation with fraudulent land sales. She'd begged him to give her details but he'd refused to say more. He had many projects and thus many people he'd partnered with and he hadn't given her a name. Instead, he told her that what he'd said and what was recorded in a Texan town would be enough, if it were ever necessary, for her to take evidence to the authorities.

What was going on? There was the sound of heavy footsteps, scuffling and another shout. Something banged above her, as if something or someone had hit the deck hard.

Besides herself, there were two other people on board. Her father and his business partner, a man she didn't know well. The arrival of Ben Whyte had been a surprise to both of them. They'd just been settling in for the night when he'd arrived on a small fishing boat. The fisherman had dropped him off and left. Neither of them had expected him. This had been their vacation—she'd sailed here to Paradise Island, Bahamas, from St. Croix with her father after he'd issued the last-minute invitation. It had been peaceful until Ben had arrived. Almost immediately, she hadn't liked the tension that Ben seemed to generate. But the initial tension between him and her father later dissolved once they began telling boisterous sports stories. She'd retired for the night as they joked about the antics of a coach on the football field. But the joking she'd left less than an hour earlier was a far cry from what she was hearing now.

Things didn't sound too friendly anymore. A curse, a series of banging and scuffling sounds that echoed through the boat. She sat up, her heart pounding.

Another shout had her tense, clenching the sheet. One foot poised on the edge of the bed as she tried to decide whether this was dream or reality. Something crashed, a hollow bang like someone had hit a wall, or the floor. The sounds escalated in volume, an angry shout followed but the words were incomprehensible.

She grabbed her phone. The thought of calling for help crowded out the other possibilities. She wasn't sure who she would be calling or why. What would the local police do about a situation that was unknown even to herself? She needed to find out what was going on, if her father needed help, if…

Footsteps thudded over her head. Their heavy tread was oddly ominous when combined with everything that had preceded them. Then something else banged, a dull sound that seemed to echo through the boat. Something had fallen and hit the deck just a little to the right of where she now sat.

"What's going on?" she muttered. She flicked on the lamp by the side of the bed. Soft light bathed the room, chasing away the shadows but not the odd noises from above deck. She got out of bed. Blindly, she grabbed something to throw on. A silk wrap that she'd pur-chased only this morning with no intention of wearing here. It was a garment made for when she had a boy-friend. It was an enticing garment. Now, it was only the first cover at hand.

She stood there for seconds. The seconds could have been a minute, maybe less, maybe more. She considered her options. But her options were unclear in a situation that was as dark as the night around her. All she knew was that something was very off. The silence that had descended in the last seconds was almost as ominous as what had preceded it. A shiver ran down her spine as she left the room. She moved through the tight passageway, slipping past the galley, which was lit only by a thin streak of moonlight that streamed through a porthole to her left. Memory guided her to the narrow metal stairs that led above deck. She was afraid to turn on any more lights, for that might alert whoever was on deck. She wouldn't think of the fact that there might be strangers, a threat of some sort aboard the yacht. Her fingers quivered and the phone shook in her damp palm.

Only a few hours earlier she had been able to see through a porthole the shadow of the shoreline. Now, there was nothing but a dark, endless stretch of water. That was odd. But even more odd was the fact that the boat was rocking as if it were on open water.

She wished she'd grabbed her slippers, for the narrow passage was chilly against her bare feet. She could only hope that what she heard was nothing, a silly argument, a bit of a wind above deck that had knocked things over. But her thoughts were stopped midstream by another crash directly above her. She jumped and bit back a scream as she dropped her phone. In the dark she couldn't see it. She felt around. Seconds passed and then a minute, maybe two. It was futile. She couldn't waste any more time searching for the phone for above her something was terribly wrong.

She took the remaining steps two at a time. She pushed open the door onto the deck. She was met by a wind that seemed to come out of nowhere and wrapped a chill breeze around her, lifting the silk from her body. She held the wrap down with one hand and pushed forward, determined to find out what was going on, to put an end to it. Seconds seemed to become minutes. She stumbled and lost her footing on the rain-slicked deck.

Her breath caught in her throat when she stepped around the wheelhouse. The moonlight lit the deck revealing two men locked together, struggling. She froze and then she took a choked breath. She covered her mouth to block the involuntary beginning of a scream.

Time seemed to stop. She could almost hear the tick of her vintage, manual-wind wristwatch as she took in details. Blood stained her father's white polo shirt. But that wasn't what frightened her the most. Instead, it was the man who stood mere inches behind her father.

The moonlight revealed the face of the man. Ben Whyte. Like her father, Ben was in his late fifties. Now it was clear that her initial feelings about the man were not misplaced. The thought pierced her shock as she put her right hand over her mouth. She couldn't believe what she was seeing.

It wasn't possible.

Her brain, her feet—everything had frozen at the shock and horror of what lay ahead of her. Things like what she was seeing only happened on television. Not to normal everyday people like her and her father. And yet she knew her father wasn't normal.

He was a wealthy philanthropist. But that wasn't the issue. Or was it?

The moonlight was glinting off the black barrel of the handgun that Ben had aimed at her father. The handgun's deadly gloss seemed to wink in the muted light of the deck. Worse, that same barrel was against her father's head. Time seemed to make the moment unendingly long when she knew that it was only seconds. She hadn't had time to think, to react, to recover from the shock. She could only watch this like it wasn't real, like it was happening to someone else. Because before she could move, her father twisted, grabbed Ben's gun hand and slammed it against the railing. Once, twice—the gun dropped and skidded across the deck.

"No! What are you doing?" Her voice seemed loud in the sudden silence. Vaguely, she realized that she hadn't shouted at all, that her cry had been no more than a whimper. She was behind and to the side of them and neither one of the men had seen or heard her. She glanced around the deck as if the answer to her father's plight lay there.

Unarmed, in bare feet and a silk wrap, with shaking hands, she was no one's hero. She looked around for a weapon, something to leverage her defense of her father. There was nothing.

Moonlight spilled over the surface of the water. She could see nothing but an endless tract of ocean around them. There was no sign of land, of Paradise Island or of the beautiful cove that they had docked in. They were in open water with no land in sight. But as much as that frightened her, the scene in front of her frightened her more.

One calamity had replaced another. Ben had her father by the throat.

"Dad!" This time the words crept past her frozen throat. This time the words weren't just her imagination. But still they were no help.

"Stay back!" Her father choked out the words with what seemed more willpower than strength, for she'd had to strain to hear him.

But rage flooded her and, despite her earlier doubts, she only knew that she had to join forces with her father. Take this threat down no matter what the odds. They could do it together, as a team—as her father always said they could. Of course, he'd meant much smaller, much less threatening situations than this. It didn't matter. This was life and death. It was, for whatever reason, them against him.

"What are you doing?" She flew at her father's attacker. The fact that the man had, a few hours ago, greeted her with all the cordiality of a long-lost friend, was now lost to her.

He was the enemy and she'd do anything in her power to stop him. Fueled by panic and a desperate kind of bravery, she grabbed his arm, trying to free her father.

"Let go!" she screeched. Her nails raked his cheek. Her actions were as desperate as she knew they were ineffective. There was no choice, there was only her and her father, who she feared would die without her help.

The punch hit her in the jaw and dropped her to her knees. She remembered nothing after that. She came in and out of consciousness. Minutes could have passed, even hours—she didn't know. The deck offered her its slick, rocking comfort as her face pressed against the cool surface.

As consciousness returned once more, the one thing that was clear was the silence. She struggled to keep her eyes open. Her head pounded and she lost consciousness again for a minute, a second—she wasn't sure.

This time when she came to she was groggy but able to sit up. As she did she saw the shadow of something against the wheelhouse. She tried to stand and slipped. Her hand caught her fall. She looked up, blinking, trying to clear her vision. She saw that Ben had somehow managed to get the pistol. But he had no chance to use it, for her father's arm came up. His arm smashed into his assailant, knocking him backward, sending the pistol flying.

"Go!" Her father waved. He glanced her way for just a second. Then, he was pulled back into a chokehold. His assailant had taken advantage of his brief distraction. Her father directed her with his eyes. Glancing to a place behind her. There was a life raft and she knew that he wanted her to leave, to leave him alone with his attacker.

"No!" she screamed, scrambling to her feet. She

clenched her fists—her hands were empty. No phone. But something else caught her eye. It was the hammer her father had used earlier to fix the back ladder. She grabbed it.

Despite her earlier failure, she wasn't willing to give up. She'd do whatever it took to help her father. She wasn't thinking straight. She was unschooled in any sort of self-defense but desperate times called for desperate measures. Her attack could confuse, muddy the waters, give her father an opening. And with that her only thought, she charged forward. She was unaware of the breeze that lifted her short sleep T-shirt revealing her upper thighs. Unaware that the silk wrap had slipped off her shoulders or that it floated behind her. Her father choked as Ben crushed his throat with one arm. But she'd caught Ben's attention, she could feel his eyes on her and that was all she needed. She'd become the distraction and hopefully by doing that give her father enough of an edge to get free. Unfortunately, she could see from the look on his face that the only thing that stood between her and rape was her father. If her father died...

Ben looked at her with eyes filled with lust. He smiled in a way that held an ugly promise, one no woman would fail to recognize and one no woman would ever want. It made her feel dirty and terrified at once. She was frightened not just for her father but for herself. Too late, she realized her mistake. She should have put something else on, anything but what she had grabbed in her panic.

She'd never trusted him. She wished she'd told her father that. But it was too late. As if killing her father wasn't enough... It wouldn't happen. Her father wasn't dead and no matter how many times she had to remind herself of that, it wouldn't happen.

She raised the hammer and brought it down, catching Ben in the shoulder. He roared, releasing his grip on her father, reaching for her.

"Dad!" she screamed as she scrambled to get away from Ben.

Her father slammed Ben's arm into the wheelhouse. He buried his fist in the man's midsection, throwing him off balance. Another punch hit him in the jaw and Ben gasped for breath. His third punch knocked Ben down.

"Run, Ava!" her father shouted and didn't give her a chance to consider before he had grabbed her hand. Together they ran, stumbling, propping each other up heading for the back of the yacht.

"Get in the life raft," he hissed in an urgent undertone. "Get out of here. I'll catch up. Once I..." His words were slurred. A tooth was broken and blood streamed from his mouth. His hair was wild and his eyes glazed. "Go." He was half lifting her over the edge of the yacht, giving her no option. She shook her head. Her fractured thoughts spun.

"Call Faisal!" her father said with a shove that had her landing in the dinghy. "Al-Nassar," he added as if she wouldn't know who he meant with just his given name. There was no other Faisal who had been in their

life. But why call him now? Then she remembered—
Nassar Security. There was no time for thoughts or
justifications—there was no time for anything. They
needed to get out of here. Already her father was undo-
ing the ropes that attached the small craft to the yacht.

"No." She couldn't leave him alone. "Come with
me!"

"This is the only way you can help me, kid." It was
the pet name he'd always used for her, and still did
despite her recent quarter-of-a-century status. He'd
teased her on her birthday about how old she was and
how old that made him.

Her eyes met his.

"Go."

"No." The word was strangled, panicked. As if she
had any choice. She was already below deck level
and had to look up. "If you stay, so do I. I won't leave
you alone."

He was so banged up. She couldn't leave him.

"I need you to go," he said firmly. "I can't be distracted trying to save you. I need to know you're safe."

It was his way of promising that he'd make it.

She knew there was nothing she could say to
change his mind. Her teeth were pressing so hard
into her lip that she tasted blood. And none of that
stopped the shaking, the fear for both of them and for
him especially.

"I'll be right behind you. I promise."

"Here." She stood up, fighting for balance as she
reached up and handed him the hammer. She had to

trust that he'd be safe. There was no help for it. He'd taken the option of choice from her. And she could see now that the life raft was so small it might sink under the weight of both of them.

He took the hammer, his fingers brushing hers, and at the same time pushed something into her hand. She didn't look but only closed her hand around the damp plastic.

"Call…" He wiped a trail of blood from his upper lip. His nose was bleeding, the blood mixing with that from his lip and trailing down his chin. "Al-Nassar. The number's there," he reminded her in a voice that was pitched only for her. Behind them she could see his assailant struggling to his feet.

"Go!" The word echoed like the needless repetition it was. She had no choice. Choice was the option that had been removed from her arsenal. Her father had decided. She would be safe and he would face… She couldn't think, didn't know. She only knew that she was alone.

"Dad…" That one word trailed, bottomless and hopeless. For there was nothing to say.

A gunshot had her on her knees with a scream as the raft rocked and threatened to tip. She clutched the rope lashed to the side. The raft settled enough that she could look up. There was no doubt that what she'd heard was a handgun. She'd heard them many times, on the firing range with her father.

Her head spun and she sat back down. When she looked up to where she had last seen her father, he was gone. Waves pushed against the side of the life raft taking it farther from the yacht. She needed to get to shore, get help. She pulled the engine cord, grimacing at the old-fashioned technology. Her father was usually the first to buy the newest and latest, except for the life raft. Its age was jarring in the scheme of everything else that was always so top-of-the-line. She yanked the cord again. Her arm ached and nothing happened.

Her father's last words seemed to spin in an endless reel through her mind.

Faisal. She had to call Faisal.

It was her last thought before she passed out in a heap in the middle of the dinghy.

BEN WASN'T SURE how it had happened. But he'd gotten lucky and landed in the water. He'd just missed hitting his head on the way down. He'd seen Dan fall overboard. But then he'd fallen in himself. It didn't matter, he'd planned to swim for shore anyway. He'd shot Dan first and he'd gone over a dead man. The yacht was on autopilot, its navigational system dead, heading somewhere out to sea. In other circumstances he might have laughed. It would keep the authorities occupied trying to find the boat.

There was only one threat left and that was the little witch of a daughter Dan had managed to dump in the life raft. There'd been nothing he could do to stop him. It had all happened so fast. He felt a twinge of regret. Now Dan was gone and the yacht was already too far away to be a consideration. He'd raised the anchor before the altercation began.

He swam toward shore. He'd locked in his mind in what direction and how far away they had drifted. Yet, the weather system was moving in faster than had been reported. It was a squall, and that and his aching shoulder had him gulping water and struggling as the weather worsened. Combine the weather with the fact that his clothes weighed him down, and it was rough going. He reached down, wrestling with the laces of his oxfords, finally managing to get them off and tie them to the belt loop of his pants. It wasn't supposed to go like this. He wished he hadn't had to kill Dan, but once he'd made the decision, he'd accomplished what he'd meant to. He'd shot Dan and he'd fallen overboard. Now there was only one problem he had to resolve before he could become a rich man. The one fly in the ointment was Dan's daughter. She wasn't supposed to be on the yacht. Yet, there she'd been like it was her right. He hadn't liked her the first and only other time he'd met her.

She'd heard too much and she'd injured him. Neither offense could be forgiven. A wave pushed him backward and had him swallowing water. He choked and flipped onto his back, resting, thinking. He had to get to shore and then he had to find Ava Adams, and when he did, the little witch had to die.

Chapter Two

The United States Coast Guard received the first distress call shortly before 0100 hours from BASRA. The acronym stood for the Bahamas Air Sea Rescue Association. A volunteer association, their resources were stretched with other cases and they were more than willing to request help. Two hours after the information was in the hands of the United States Coast Guard, that information was relayed to the Wyoming branch of Nassar Security.

It had taken that long for the connection between the owner of the yacht, Dan Adams, and Sheik Faisal Al-Nassar to be made. The connection came from the yacht owner's electronic log that had also provided their last location off the coast of Paradise Island. Dan Adams had included in the log his next destination and purpose. A meeting in Fort Lauderdale with Faisal Al-Nassar.

Faisal was told that the call for help was made on

a cell phone. The call lasted exactly nine seconds and then had broken off and been too short to trace. It had been a male caller who had provided only two words, *Mayday* and *Ava*. Ava was Dan's stepdaughter's name and the other person aboard that yacht. There was no record of anyone else being on the yacht. The call had ended immediately after that.

Faisal couldn't believe that the father and daughter were missing. He was reminded of how long it had been since he'd spoken to Ava. While her father had remained in contact, he and Ava had lost touch. Still, the father and daughter were considered friends of the family. Now if it had been possible, Faisal would have left to begin the search immediately. But not only did he have to get to the Jackson, Wyoming, airport where they kept the company jet, the pilot had to ready himself and the craft for takeoff. They followed the twenty-minute rule. That was how long it took the pilot to prepare for takeoff.

Faisal glanced at his snowboard with regret. He'd just hung it up after waxing it and preparing it for a trip to Mount Hood in Oregon where there was enough snow to board throughout the year. Now that would have to wait. The thoughts of snowboarding were only a way of grounding himself, by thinking of what he loved, before being immersed in a case that was much too personal.

He brought his attention to the immediate as he called his brother Emir. Emir, the oldest in their family and the head of Nassar Security, was located in their head office, which was situated in Marrakech, Morocco. He knew without question that he could count on Emir to relay the plight of their old friend to the rest of the Al-Nassar family.

"Dan and Ava are lost at sea. The US Coast Guard is deployed as is the Bahamas Air Sea Rescue Association. Of course, the latter is volunteer. I'm on wing to fly to Florida," he said abruptly when Emir answered.

"What happened?" Emir asked. "They were on vacation. Last I heard they…" The words ended on an expletive.

"The yacht was last seen just off the coast of Paradise Island, Bahamas. It's since disappeared off the radar. When I spoke to Dan, he said he was heading to Fort Lauderdale earlier than planned. We had a meeting set up. A change of plans and then they disappear. Is there a connection?" Faisal asked. There was a raw edge to his voice that he made no effort to mute. "Look, I've got a plane to catch, I'll keep you posted."

"I'll let the rest of the family know. Dan stuck by us when everyone else thought expanding the business to the United States was a crazy idea. We'll stick by him now."

"Definitely," Faisal said, remembering all Dan had done. The Al-Nassars were an old and revered family in Morocco and Nassar Security was an established business in Marrakech. His family had been anxious to expand and it was partially because of Dan, who had lived in Wyoming at the time, that they had chosen that state. The rest, he knew, had been his own doing. He'd pushed the envelope with his siblings. He loved Wyoming and the wide open spaces. It was where he'd finished his degree. Fresh out of university, he'd been eager to be part of the new venture, especially if he could convince his siblings to choose Wyoming…and he had. He'd loved the new branch from the beginning, particularly because of the challenge. He'd known that in Wyoming his name and status as Sheik Faisal Al-Nassar would not open doors like it did at home. The idea had challenged and excited him. And despite the obstacles, his brothers had agreed—they'd all welcomed the challenge. And so Nassar Security had expanded. Dan had been a mentor to him in the early years.

During that first year of getting a footing in a new country, Dan had been the father that Faisal had lost too young. He shook his head as if that would dislodge memories. He'd never forget how special Dan Adams was to their family. Nor, despite losing touch with her, did he forget how special his daughter had once been to him. In fact, he was reeling more from knowing that Ava too was now considered lost at sea. His mind kept going back to the dark-haired beauty. He'd spent his last year of university with her. He remembered the jokes, the teasing and the parties, and he remembered something else—how she had made him feel.

Three hours later, from one of the Nassar Gulfstream jets, Faisal looked out the window. It was dark and cloudy in the minutes before the sun began to rise.

His mind went beyond what he could see to the Atlantic where two people he cared for were now missing.

According to the United States Coast Guard, there had been only one call for help. It was thought to have come from the Adamses' yacht as that was the only vessel reported missing. They had heard a name but the call had disconnected. There hadn't been enough to give them a location, nothing. All they had was the name Ava spoken in a male voice.

He pushed back a strand of hair that seemed to have a mind of its own. He should get it cut but there never seemed to be enough time. He'd tried it short but that hadn't lasted. Ava had once told him that she loved his hair just over the tips of his earlobes and longer if he'd consider it. The latter wasn't a consideration but the former had stuck in his mind. He'd met her during his senior year in university and they'd become friends. They'd both grown up since then and gone their own ways. That part of his life was long over. At least that's what he told himself. Except today. He was again faced with the truth. He'd never forgotten her.

"We'll find them," he said in an undertone as if saying the words made them somehow more real. Maybe the words made his doubts of success smaller. While the Bahamas were close to the continental United States there was still a lot of ocean to cover. Without coordinates of any kind, they had only guesswork. Despite that and maybe because of it, he was not going to sit around waiting. Dan had planned to see him in

Fort Lauderdale—it was up to him to make sure that meeting happened.

His thoughts went back to the last phone call.

Based on what they knew, the Adamses could be anywhere. They were no longer close to Paradise Island's shoreline. A search by the Bahamas Air Sea Rescue Association had already exhausted that option. Wherever they were, whatever had happened, the answers were on that yacht.

AVA ADAMS OPENED her eyes. Her head ached and something deep inside her hurt. That hurt was overshadowing the thumping that seemed to want to break her skull. Yet it wasn't pain. Not a physical pain but something more emotional. Fear. Anger. She didn't know what. Instead, she shivered. She was alone and she wasn't on the yacht. Where was she?

The yacht was gone. She had no idea what had happened to either it or her father. It had disappeared while she'd slipped out of consciousness. She had no idea how long she'd been unconscious. Nothing held any relevance, not time nor space—nor anything that had happened. All of it was a frightening blur.

The breeze ran light, cool fingers across her damp skin and she shivered. She didn't know how long she'd been unconscious, all she knew was that she was alone and there was no land in sight. Her head pounded and her vision was blurred. She couldn't see clearly no matter how hard she tried. She was fighting to remain conscious so that she could make that promised call to get help. Her father was counting on her.

The thought made her prop herself up despite her shaking limbs. She tried not to look at the dark water. There was only a thin layer of rubber and canvas between her and it. She couldn't think of it any more than she could contemplate the fate of her father. All she knew was that the yacht was gone and with it her father. She didn't know when it had disappeared or if her father was on board or if he was even alive. She struggled to sit up and the world spun. She took a deep breath and passed out.

The next time she came to, she could see that the sun was higher in the sky. It was behind her and she guessed that she might be heading west. She had no idea what that might mean about where she would end up. Or if she would end up anywhere except maybe at the bottom of the ocean.

Fear threatened to overwhelm her even as her gut knotted along with her fists. Her head spun and she had to fight not to black out again. She needed to think and yet she was fighting not to lose consciousness again. She needed to get help not just for her but for her father. He needed her. He was alone.

That thought collided with another. Was her father alive? She'd heard the gunshot as the life raft had slipped away from the yacht, carried by the ocean current. There had been silence after that as she'd drifted farther away.

The gunshot had echoed long after the actual event.

The haunting reminder was like an omen. She could die out here and her father could already be dead. Those scenarios were ones she couldn't, wouldn't consider. Not anymore. She refused to think of him as anything but alive—just as she was determined to reach land, one way or another.

She took a deep breath and again she fought to sit up. The life raft rocked, threatening what stability it had as water sloshed in the bottom. She wasn't sure how it had taken on water unless it had been in those first moments as it had gone from the yacht to sea. The sea had been rough. It hadn't calmed much since then. It was cloudy and the breeze was picking up, only a bit of sun peeked through the otherwise dreary sky.

She had nothing. She looked down. She was virtually naked. The skimpy sleeping outfit had been a bad choice. Fortunately, her father had thrown his jacket over her. Who would have known that a trip that had begun as a lark would end like this?

It wouldn't end.

Determination shot through her chilled body. She had too much to do with her life. She had a new career that had yet to begin. Again she repeated that promise to herself and to her father. They would live. He would live. They had to.

Something cold pressed against her hip. She slipped her hand under the waistband of her panties and pulled out her father's phone. She'd forgotten it was there.

Her heart stopped. She remembered that he'd handed it to her. It was a miracle that it had not dropped to the bottom of the dinghy, into the water that was gathering there.

She held it, the memory of her father handing it to her clear in her mind.

"Call Faisal."

She knew, as did her father, that if anyone could help them, it was Faisal. He headed the powerhouse investigative company run by his family, Nassar Security. At least he was in charge of their Wyoming branch.

The phone slipped in her damp hands.

"SHEIK FAISAL," SHE MURMURED. It was an odd thing to say, to even think. But in the chaos and panic of what had happened, she vaguely remembered what now seemed like so long ago. It had been her senior year of college when she'd first met Faisal. He'd transferred in for that last year. He'd been two years older but she'd been two years ahead of her grade. She'd skipped through grade school in six years instead of eight and skipped kindergarten altogether. Although, the latter didn't count, she'd been the standard age when she'd entered first grade. Odd memories drifted through her mind. Just the mention of his name brought everything back. She couldn't move, could only fight to remain conscious and all the while she remembered. She'd teased him about his title of Sheik, and he'd hated having it mentioned. It was strange the places her mind wanted to go when there was so little time. Consciousness could slip away as easily as it had returned.

She gripped the phone with the desperation of the survivor she now was. The phone and a man who had once been a friend, who she had once hoped would be more than just friend, were now her only hope.

The sun beamed down through a break in the clouds and instead of offering hope it only reminded her of the passage of time. It was a reminder that her and her father's chances of survival decreased with every moment that passed.

She swallowed heavily—the world was graying and beginning to spin. She shut her eyes, focusing on one thing, on remaining conscious at least long enough to get help, to contact someone, to...

Everything blanked out.

She didn't know for how long or what had happened in the time between awareness and when she opened her eyes again. Like before, all she could see was the ocean. She was in the middle of nowhere and drifting to who knew where. If she thought about it too much she might fall into the abyss and succumb to panic. Her hand slid on the slick bottom of the dingy where water was pooling and was now a quarter inch deep. She could sink if this continued. She took a deep breath. She had to remain calm.

She looked at the phone. It was still in her hand. Had it been there all along? How long had she been out this time? She couldn't remember. It didn't matter. What mattered was that no more time passed before she called. She pushed a button and the phone's screen lit up.

"Thank goodness," she said in a whisper with what seemed the last bit of strength she had. The wind pushed the struggling life raft in a half circle. As the raft shifted direction, she shivered. She didn't know how long she could stay afloat or where she was. She was dizzy, fighting to stay awake. She had to do this. She clutched the phone as if it were a lifeline, and in a way it was.

She looked at the screen, squinting as her vision blurred. Everything seemed to spin and then stop.

"No," she whispered. She couldn't afford to pass out, not before she made this call. Her stomach clenched and her hands shook harder at what was in front of her. But there was no changing the fact that the battery icon was red. Her hand shook harder. She needed to phone now, while there was still some power left. Instead she fainted.

When she came to, the phone was in her lap. She remembered the battery life as if that frightening fact had been etched in her mind. Hopefully there was some juice left and it wasn't too late. She knew this was her only chance. Without the phone, without this call and a connection there was nothing. Nothing but a hunk of rubber slowly taking on water stood between her and… She couldn't think of it. She had to remain positive. She had to get hold of Faisal. Her father's voice telling her to do that wouldn't leave her head. He'd suggested no one else, just Faisal.

She couldn't focus, yet she desperately wanted this horror to end. Despite that or because of it, she remembered another time, another place. Faisal. She'd been on the cusp of adulthood and he'd been her everything for such a short time. Now, again he was her everything but in such a different way. He was all that stood between her and death, between her father and death. This time she was counting on him like she never had before.

She took in a shaky breath, pushed herself gingerly up and opened the contacts. She hit Faisal's number and the screen went black. The battery had run out along with every chance she'd ever had.

Her world started to spin. She tried to force herself to keep conscious and she couldn't. She slumped sideways as she blacked out. Her last thought was that she was on her own and she didn't stand a chance. But then the phone hiccupped back to life.

Chapter Three

Saturday, June 11—9:00 a.m.

It had been more than eight hours since the US Coast Guard had received the call from the missing yacht. And despite the time that had passed, they couldn't pinpoint where the yacht was. They assumed that the vessel's AIS, Automatic Identification System, a standardized system that would provide the identity, type, position, course, speed, navigational status and other safety-related facts about the vessel, was compromised. Whether that was due to criminal intent or was accidental was yet to be determined.

Faisal had checked the coordinates between Paradise Island and the continental United States. So much could affect the outcome. If it was foul play, that would change everything. If they were suffering engine failure, it could again change everything. And if they were moving under their own steam—doubtful—again, it changed everything. But with nothing to go on, they had to start somewhere.

He glanced over at Craig Vale, the only one of the Nassar team to make this trip with him. Craig was heading north after this to New York to meet up with other members of the tech team. But in the meantime, it was nice to have a researcher on the case. That so rarely happened. They were usually a distant voice via a phone or computer connection.

Faisal shifted his thoughts, focusing on what was ahead. He didn't like any of it. He was flying into a no-win situation. Yet, despite that, this was what he did and what he thrived on. He might not like it but his adrenaline was kicking in. The personal connection would no longer be at the forefront. In order for this mission to be successful he had to lead with his head, not his heart. It was no different than when his sister, Tara, had been kidnapped. He'd let his oldest brother lead the charge and he'd done the hardest thing he'd ever done in his life. He'd stayed here, managing their business thousands of miles away from that heartache. In the end, that decision had been the right one. Tara was home and safe.

He dropped the thoughts from his mind. Now, his mind was solely on this case. Rehashing probabilities and possibilities would get him nowhere. In a way, taking the thoughts from his mind, focusing on what was important, was like meditation, which was something he utilized at the beginning of every case. It was a practice he shared with his oldest brother, Emir, and Emir's wife, Kate, who had introduced him to it. It was something his whole family now practiced. It had made both their business and their family stronger and tighter as a result.

Thoughts of meditation fled as his phone beeped. It was only a notification that they were minutes from landing. He looked out the window of the private jet. Traveling by private jet was one of the many perks that came from wealth. It was also one of many he didn't give much consideration to. If asked, he would have admitted that he was privileged, lucky in the manner of his birth. It wasn't something he ever discussed or thought about. It was a fact that had always been. That part of his life, his family's inherited wealth and status, had been unchanging. He'd been born into wealth that had accrued over generations. It was what he'd always known. But it was this part, Nassar Security and his position as head of the Wyoming branch, that allowed him to play out his dreams of adventure. He couldn't imagine that anyone had a better life and there wasn't a day that he wasn't grateful.

Today was different. Today he faced a tragedy that could touch every member of his family. His phone rang, breaking into his thoughts. He froze and his heart leaped despite his training, which usually allowed him to maintain a cool facade. He held the phone for a split second for Craig to see. It wasn't a number he recognized. What unknown caller would phone now? He didn't believe in coincidence and yet he answered, praying to hear Dan's or Ava's voice.

Silence and something else. There was a sound that was as recognizable as it was disturbing. It was the sound of waves lapping against a dock or the bow of a boat.

Craig nodded, his blond ponytail bobbing where it skimmed over his collar. His nod confirmed the suspicion they had both had. His full pouty lips seemed at odds with a strong jaw. It was as if nature hadn't been sure if it was creating a tough guy or pretty boy. Either way, these conflicting traits belied his thirty-five years and made him look more like twenty.

They both held their breath, hoping the connection would hold, that they could get a trace.

"Hello," he repeated. "Dan?" There was nothing, only silence. The only surety they had was Craig's confirmation that this was Dan's number, but was it Dan? What were the odds that the search would begin on a lucky note? On finding a survivor before they'd even landed?

"Who are you? Tell me." He kept talking, hoping to keep the connection going.

He could hear something that sounded like the crash of a wave. It was different from the first one. This time it was rather like when one wave rolls down into another that is just building to a crest. It was a sound he was familiar with having spent time on a yacht with his family as a child.

He listened closely. He barely dared to breathe, as if even that might drown out other sounds, other clues. He heard what sounded like a soft breath. It wasn't much but what he'd heard sounded feminine. Feminine and indistinguishable.

The sound of water, the pattern of waves and the call of a seagull. Then there was nothing, only silence.

"Hello." He wasn't willing to give up. "Ava? Dan?" He didn't know if it was either of them. He was only taking a chance and betting on the odds against the fact that it could be anyone else. There'd been two people registered as leaving the dock in that boat.

He glanced at his watch and then over at Craig. As if to confirm his faith in him, Craig nodded and gave a thumbs-up less than a minute after the connection broke.

"I have the coordinates," Craig said.

Forty minutes later they landed. He left Craig to his own devices as he transferred to a sea rescue helicopter.

"I'd say it was good to see you, but unfortunately I can't—the circumstances suck," the pilot, Jer Keller, said. They'd flown together on a number of rescues. Jer was the same age as Faisal. He had married young and already had twin toddlers with his childhood sweetheart. But despite the differences in their home life, they both shared a passion for this. If Nassar Security hadn't existed, Faisal would have chosen a career in sea rescue. Getting the opportunity to be involved, as rare as it was, was usually a thrill. Not this time.

"At least we have hope that someone lived." He shook his head. Somehow the way he had pronounced those words sounded grim.

Sam Sanders, a blond man in his midforties, came

up to them and shook each of their hands. He was an early retiree from the Coast Guard, an experienced member of Search and Rescue who had helped out as winchman in previous rescues.

"Sam," Faisal said and clapped his hand on the man's shoulder. "Wish we met under better circumstances."

Sam nodded in his quiet, rather stoic way. "Hopefully we'll be successful and you'll have use of me." It was pretty much the last thing he said for the duration of the flight.

They'd been in the air for five minutes when Faisal moved to the back where the side doors were open.

"Better view or just being hopeful?" Jer asked through his mic.

"Both," he said. There was no way to predict how this was going to turn out despite his hopes. All he knew was that there was a storm brewing. Already the air seemed heavier, more humid. It was the intensity of the feeling, not the humidity, that reminded him of home, of Marrakech. But it had been a long time since he'd been home for anything more than a short visit. Wyoming was home now and humidity wasn't an issue. Not like here. He could feel the air, thick and difficult to breath. He loved the feel of open spaces, the small population, the sweeping plains and the blessed winter. The congestion of a city like Miami or the one of his birth, Marrakech, overwhelmed his senses. He'd known that since he was a boy. It was the reason why, for almost the last decade, he'd lived in

Wyoming. It was a vast state with a sparse population that fit his personality like nothing else. He loved the town of Jackson. It was small, a good place to dig in one's heels. He could never imagine going back. Big cities were fun in the moment but anything more than a day or two and he was antsy. Unfortunately he was here in Miami for as long as it took to solve this case.

They'd been flying for well over an hour. Jer and he had caught up on where each of them were in their lives. For five minutes they flew in silence.

"Do you see it?" Jer asked.

"I do." He was hanging half out of the chopper. Ahead of them and slightly less than fifty miles off the coast of Paradise Island was a speck that didn't fit. A minute later and it was clear that it was a small dark gray dinghy.

"Bang on, Craig," he said as if the tech was actually present. His coordinates had been near perfect, for the craft was only a mile away from where his tech had tracked it. It was barely visible as it rose and fell in waves that were growing larger with every minute.

"Raft," Jer said unnecessarily as he read off the coordinates. "We may have us a survivor."

The helicopter buzzed closer and it was hard to tell who or what they might be faced with. Faisal could only hope that there were at least two people in that life raft, the right two people—Dan and Ava Adams.

Tension mixed with excitement settled within the confines of the helicopter. The odds that this could be anyone else, considering even what little they knew, were remote.

"It's loaded," Jer said as he dipped the helicopter and lost altitude.

His gaze swept the area while never letting the life raft leave his sight. Dan and Ava had to be alive. He refused to accept another scenario. He looked at his watch as he estimated the hours they might have been in the water.

Faisal got into position to be dropped down. The flight suit he'd donned an hour earlier seemed both familiar and restrictive. He should have a wetsuit but he hadn't thought of that. Emotion had blinded him. He wiped perspiration from his forehead and let the adrenaline fire him up as it always did.

"One occupant," Faisal muttered a few minutes later as he slipped the harness on and prepared to be dropped. His heart sank. That meant that one of them might not have made it.

He wasn't going to assume anything. This could be Ava Adams or Dan Adams or it could even be someone else who had been on that yacht, someone he wasn't aware of. For now, he was focused on rescue, nothing more.

Whoever was in the raft hadn't moved. And it was impossible to tell from this distance if they were alive or dead.

Chapter Four

"We've got a survivor." Jer's overly enthusiastic voice seemed oddly disembodied as it came through the headset.

Faisal didn't respond, not even to the whoop that followed Jer's statement. Neither were something that needed a response. Neither the enthusiasm nor the words that preceded it needed confirmation. They had all seen, as the waves rocked the raft, the movement within the small craft. But the move had been slight and gave no indication as to the condition of their survivor. Those thoughts ran through his mind as he focused on the details of his descent.

Sam turned and gave him a thumbs-up.

Faisal returned the gesture feeling pumped and optimistic.

The ocean was rough and the raft was clearly visible now. In fact, they were close enough to see that the survivor was alone, and that she was no longer moving. They could also see that her feet were bare. Her peach-colored wrap barely covered her torso and was the only spot of color against the dark gray craft and the stormy gray of the ocean only hinting at blue. Her dark hair spread like tangled clumps of seaweed around her. Her body seemed to rock with the movement of the water, rising and falling, offering no resistance. It was as if she were barely alive and, despite the movement they'd seen minutes earlier, that they might be too late.

Faisal pushed that thought away. He was poised at the open doorway, wanting to move into action.

"She looks in rough shape," Jer said as he turned the helicopter around, bringing it closer to the raft. He cleared his throat. They both knew that despite Jer's earlier enthusiasm, which was so typical of him, that what he said now only reflected his doubt that they had a survivor at all.

"We'll get her to Mercy in Miami."

"I'll let them know the status and give the Coast Guard a heads-up too."

"Possible survivor," he said for Jer's benefit so that he could relay the information. He only prayed it was true. If it were, they'd got here in the nick of time. She was in the middle of nowhere and way underdressed for the overnight conditions. Water in the life raft was causing it to list and that only caused more waves to crest the top of the small craft and fill it with more water. It was only a matter of time before this life raft sank.

They were closer now and it was clearer than it had been earlier that she wasn't dead. She'd moved.

It had only been a slight, maybe involuntary action because she'd been still since but it was movement. Relief raced through him while at the same time he wished more than just the three of them were here to rescue her. If they'd had time they would have brought a medic with them. But the timing had been off and the swiftness with which they'd had to move out had prevented any of that. The only thing they could do was make tracks to the emergency room.

It was a fairly easy descent. What wasn't going to be easy was the landing. It wasn't something he'd done in a while but it wasn't unfamiliar, none of it was, not the work nor the pilot he was currently working with. Jer and he had worked together before many times and, despite his idiosyncrasies, he was one of the best.

Minutes later he was lowering himself toward the raft. He waved at Sam once as he gave a direction before twisting in the wind churned up by the helicopter blades. He angled toward the raft as much as he could but the conditions were against him. The wind was kicking up faster than he'd anticipated. The life raft was rocking in the waves. Despite Jer's expertise in keeping the helicopter in position, and Sam's with the winch line, it was taking all his skill to keep on target.

Already, he could see that this rescue was going to be much more difficult than they'd thought. They'd factored in as much as they could. While the wind had been part of that, there was no correcting for the force of the wind twisting him as he descended. That combined with a rough ocean had both the weather and the raft working against them. She'd moved only once since that slight movement almost ten minutes ago when they'd first spotted her. Had both times only been a figment of his imagination? Had it been only the result of the freefall of the raft as it fell within the trough of the waves? Yet he'd factored that, and they hadn't thought so at the time. Still, he wondered.

Dark hair streamed down her back. He was close enough now to see that she was slim and long legged, and while he shouldn't be sure without seeing her face, he knew without doubt who she was. And his heart pounded in response to that knowing.

He wanted to hurry the last few seconds up, get on the raft. But he couldn't rush, couldn't afford a mistake. Instead he took in details, as if that would take the edge off his impatience. She had little on, a silk cover that was soaked and covered nothing. What looked like a man's jacket was draped over her ankles like it had slipped down during the night. Her face was hidden from him by her hair. That was a concern for she was lying facedown. She could have suffocated against the rubber or drowned in the water that covered some of the bottom of the dinghy.

Ava. It had to be her. But if it was, this wasn't how he'd imagined their reunion. This wasn't how he'd imagined her at all. It had been five years since he'd seen her. She'd texted him a couple of times and he'd texted back and then they'd both gotten caught up in their own lives. They'd been friends and yet there'd been something else there. They'd both felt it and yet they'd never acted on it.

Ava. He'd never forgotten her.

It was odd to be thinking such things in the dark heart of a rescue. All his attention should be focused on landing in rough seas. Normally he would have focused but nothing about this situation was normal. His feet tentatively touched the edge of the raft and then lifted off. It was too small. He didn't know if it would hold both of them.

He had to try.

She moved.

Even in the awkward position he was in, relief shot through him. The wind twisted him yet again and he fought to come in at the right angle, to position himself with feet on the raft, not in the water. Either way, he'd get to her, but getting wet wasn't in his plan. At least, it wasn't the option he'd choose.

He pushed those thoughts aside. He needed to concentrate on the task ahead of him. He was hanging just over the life raft. As he determined how much of his weight the small vessel could take, she turned onto her side and opened her eyes. He put his foot down on the rubber to stop a slight spin. It was the last thing he did for over half a minute as he was caught in a memory he'd thought was long forgotten. It had been a youthful connection replaced by the reality called life and the space of five years. But the depths of those blue eyes reminded him that he'd never forgotten. The connection was brief. She closed her eyes again with a sigh as if she knew that she was safe even as she slipped back into unconsciousness. He couldn't waste time looking at her pale face or the full lips that were almost as pallid as the porcelain skin of her slim neck. There wasn't time to consider anything—she needed to get medical help. He went over her with quick hands and eyes. He made sure that there wasn't any injury that needed immediate attention, no blood or awkward positioning of limbs. There was nothing except an unnatural stillness that meant she'd slipped back into unconsciousness. A pass of his hand beneath her nostrils told him that she continued to breathe.

He had to get her into the helicopter and to the hospital as quickly as possible. The mysteries of why she was here and where her father was would have to remain just that. The US Coast Guard, the Bahamas Air Sea Rescue Association and a swarm of volunteers were searching the waters for the yacht. Hopefully Dan Adams was still on board and there'd be answers. If they found the yacht without him, despite having found Ava, the chances of succeeding twice were slim. The Atlantic was a big place and even now the waves were rough with weather reports saying it wasn't going to get any better. His focus returned to where Ava Adams lay unmoving with nothing but six square feet of air-inflated rubber to protect her from the elements. She wasn't even wearing a life jacket. That reality horrified him as he thought of all the possibilities and of how lucky she'd been. The Ava he knew was a poor swimmer. If she'd ended up in the water, she would have drowned in waves like this. She'd been lucky he'd arrived when he had.

It was five minutes before he had her harnessed and buckled against him. It had been awkward trying to balance on the dinghy and maneuver her into the harness. Now, he held her tight against his chest, his arm around her, her breasts pressed against his chest. It seemed inappropriate and wrong. And yet all he could do was hold one arm over the harness that held her and the other a safe distance away as he held the winch line. He looked up and signaled Sam to take them up. The roar of the helicopter blades and the crash of the waves below them made communicating impossible. The line twisted, and they turned, facing away from the empty life raft as the line slowly took them up.

She moaned and it was odd hearing her voice for the first time in so long. She opened her eyes. He hadn't expected that nor her unseeing gaze. It was as unexpected as the first time. This time her eyes held nothing but desperation and panic.

"Find my father." Her words were so low and breathy. It was like it took all her energy just to breathe.

"We will," he said. He held her tighter, her body damp and cold, and her curves pressed into him, teasing him in ways that he could not ignore.

His thoughts were blown away with her next words.

"He'll kill him."

Chapter Five

He'll kill him.

With Ava safely in the helicopter, her words still echoed in his mind. Unfortunately, after that cryptic statement, she'd passed out. There was no clue as to who she might be referring to. The yacht had officially held two passengers, Dan Adams and Ava. Did someone want them dead? And if so, who?

They hadn't arrived a moment too soon.

Getting her into the helicopter was difficult, getting her on the stretcher, no easier. She'd been limp, and because of that, dead weight. She'd floated back into unconsciousness for a while after he'd gotten her into the helicopter and before he'd pulled up the rescue gear. A few minutes, not a whole lot more.

She grimaced and then squinted as if she couldn't focus. She wasn't looking at anything; in fact, her eyes were half-closed and hidden by long dark lashes. Her eyes opened a little wider but again remained unfocused on either him or anything else.

He remembered those eyes so full of intelligence

and passion. He remembered the vivid blue piercing challenge of them and he remembered the vulnerability behind her shrewd intellect. Despite what he'd told himself over the years, he'd forgotten nothing about her. He pushed the thoughts from his mind. Irrelevant. He needed to keep her safe, get her warm and get her to the hospital.

The only assessment he could make was that she didn't seem to be seeing him. She wasn't looking at him or around him—instead it was as if she didn't see him or anything else at all. It was like she was asleep with her eyes open.

"What happened, Ava?" he asked in an undertone. Sam had moved from the winch just behind him up to the copilot seat beside Jer. Faisal was alone with Ava. Her misty blue gaze seemed to float past him, not taking him in or even her surroundings. She seemed to slip in and out of awareness. Her moments of lucidity were sometimes just moments of opening her eyes. She was unfocused as if nothing was part of her reality. He didn't expect an answer. He wasn't sure why he had asked the question. She was in a fragile state but at least now she had a chance. He hoped that they could say the same about her father, Dan Adams.

"Dad," she whispered as she closed her eyes. But that one word wasn't an answer, it only raised more questions.

"No, Ava. It's me, Faisal." He looked at the face that he remembered so well. The high cheekbones were pale, taut over the bones of her face. A few freckles that he hadn't known she had seemed to stand out against her pale skin. There was so little that had changed and yet so much. She'd been twenty the last time he'd seen her and he'd been twenty-two. For the majority of the years since then, he'd headed the Wyoming branch of Nassar Security. He hadn't forgotten Ava. He'd gone one way and she'd gone another. She'd continued with her schooling. He'd heard from Emir only weeks ago that she'd graduated with a PhD in psychology. Life had happened to them and their friendship had slipped under the radar for a time.

There had always been the promise of something more. But she'd been too young and he'd been with someone else. They'd been friends but always there had been the hint of something more. In another time, if he had been wiser things might have been different.

Seconds later, she opened her eyes. He was startled, for it looked like she had been crying. As if she knew, even in her half-conscious state, that she'd been the sole survivor. She closed her eyes again without having focused on him or on anything else in the chopper. It was like she was there and yet wasn't.

"How's she doing?" Jer asked.

"In and out of consciousness," he said.

"He killed him," she murmured a few minutes later as she opened and then again closed her eyes.

There was no point asking who. Sooner or later she would come to and then she would remember and be able to tell him what had happened. If it was too much later, they would find the information by other means.

He pulled another blanket over her. He reached for a third, rolled it and put it under her calves, thus elevating her legs. At least the fact that she'd shivered was evidence that she hadn't fallen too far into her unconscious state.

He needed to get some heat on her. More important, he knew that he had to get her out of the wet clothes that clung to her skin. The wet material was only chilling her even further and making the blanket useless. He pulled the blankets back, using one of them to shield what he could of her body. He peeled away the flimsy material. Her skin was damp. He tried to preserve her modesty. But there was only so much he could do. He left her panties on. They were damp too but what he'd done had been enough. At least she wouldn't arrive in the emergency room completely naked. Not that it mattered, but yet it did matter and he wasn't sure why. He tucked another blanket around her.

He put a hand on Ava's forehead. The contact sent a tingle through his hand as if there were still a connection between them. But there was nothing, all of that was over. It was stupid of him to think of that. Silly to remember something that had been nothing but a flirtatious friendship despite what he had wanted. It had been a long time ago. They were different people. He was sure she'd changed, much as he had. He regretted not following up with her. If he had then he'd know who she'd become, what had happened to the happy girl with the quick wit. He took his attention to the immediate. She was warm. There was a sheen to her forehead, like a fever might be developing. Her forehead was moist and not, he knew, from her time in the dinghy. He hoped she didn't have a fever but the heat he was feeling didn't bode well. It didn't matter. They would get her to the hospital and she'd be fine. It was the location of her father that was more disconcerting. For his fate was unknown.

"Dad," she murmured.

This time there was expectation in the way she said the word, as if she thought her father might make an appearance.

"Find my father," she said in a breathy whisper.

"It's Faisal," he said, hoping that his voice might somehow bring her back to consciousness.

He leaned closer. "You're alright." It wasn't a question but a statement meant to reassure her, to let her know that she was no longer alone.

She pushed him away but it was barely a tap as her one hand dropped and her other didn't even lift. Nor did she open her eyes. Her head moved to the side as if she were trying to do more but was too weak. "Kill..."

"What?" Sam asked.

"What the hell?" Jer's voice came through the headset. "What's she talking about? Kill who, what?"

"I wish I knew," Faisal said. His attention never left her face. But Ava had closed her eyes again as if that one disturbing word was too much. "Maybe something about what she's been through. Maybe nothing."

"Nothing. I doubt that," Jer replied. "*Kill* is a fairly intense word in any context."

"True," Faisal agreed.

"I've been in contact with Miami's Mercy Hospital. They're the closest and they're expecting us." Jer's voice came over his earpiece. "Contacted Search and Rescue too. They'll pass the info on that we've found Ava Adams."

Below, the ocean swept out around them but there was no sign of the missing yacht nor was there any sign of land. Wherever Dan Adams was, they could only hope he was alive and could hang on. The horizon stretched out in front of them and seemed to mock the fact that help was now minutes away.

BEN WHYTE ROLLED over and moaned. The sun was glaring in his eyes and he couldn't stand to look at it. He'd dragged himself to shore in the wee hours of the night. He'd lost track of time during a swim that had seemed to go on forever. He hadn't realized that he'd been that far from shore. It was all supposed to be so much easier than it actually had been. The dispute and resulting fight should never have happened.

Dan Adams, he thought with disdain. The man was an idiot. He hadn't thought so only days ago, but it was clear now. Dan had signed his own death certificate by admitting what he knew and then confronting him with it. The Dan of the past would never have done that. He would have silently turned him in.

He looked behind him where he could see the distant rise of Paradise Island hotels and other high-rises. But on this strip of sand there was nothing. He needed to ferry over to the main island where the cruise ships were. From there he could slip on the below deck crew entrance on a ship heading for Florida. His hand slid into his pocket and pulled out a debit card and a small wad of soggy bills. He was taking a chance but he could use the card to get a ticket on the ferry.

He guesstimated that he'd swum for well over an hour before collapsing on this stretch of sand and passing out exhausted for the rest of the night. The only thing motivating him to stay alive was the fact that there was too much at stake for him to die. He was one transaction away from being a rich man and that idiot Dan Adams had almost ruined it all, him and his damn daughter. The meddlesome little witch.

He'd needed Dan. His reputation in their partnership was gold. The land didn't exist, at least not land owned by him, but by the time the damn foreigners found out about it, it would be too late. Except Dan wanted to pull out of the partnership.

He'd shown up on the yacht to give Dan one more chance. Ava Adams was never supposed to have been on board. Dan had told him he was going on a yachting vacation and he hadn't mentioned his daughter. Instead he'd mentioned the fact that his daughter had accepted a position—her first job. Supposedly it started in some forsaken Wyoming town in the next week or two. He'd forgotten the details. It had only amazed him at the time. Amazed him that anyone would want to live in that backwater. But she'd gone to school there and had been forever infatuated with Wyoming. All that aside, he'd never expected to see her. He'd never thought that she'd fly down to join her father. Dan had never mentioned the possibility.

His hand slid to his waist. Empty. He'd been armed at the beginning of this. Dan had hit him and for a minute his world had grayed and then, when he'd come to, he'd shot him and seen Dan fall overboard.

Now, Ava Adams, if she survived, at best she knew he'd killed her father, at worst she knew it all. He had no idea what her father had told her. What he did know was that he needed to close his last deal before the truth came out. But his Canadian buyer was already showing suspicion and reluctant to pay the balance of what he owed for that tract of land he was so hot to have. Time was of the essence, for he'd heard both impatience and a hint of disbelief in their last phone call. It was as if the buyer had lost confidence in the deal, in Ben's ability to facilitate the transfer. It was as if he sensed the truth. That couldn't happen, for the truth would destroy everything. Even without Dan's reputation backing him, he planned to close this deal. There was too much money at stake. One word from Dan's daughter and it would be over before he had a chance to leave. He needed that last payout and he needed it desperately. He couldn't chance the possibility that Ava Adams would reveal what she knew.

She needed to be dealt with immediately. But

the grim reaper wouldn't deal out death by sleight of hand. If she wasn't dead yet, in order for her to die, he needed a gun.

Chapter Six

The flight to Mercy Hospital in Miami seemed to take forever. During the time in the air, Ava Adams had gotten worse. Her breathing was shallow. She hadn't regained consciousness since Faisal had stripped most of her wet clothes from her and wrapped her in thermal blankets. She wasn't shivering anymore but she wasn't moving either.

Now, seeing her like this, flirting with death the way she was, was killing him. It was like reliving another dark time when the life of someone he'd loved had been in jeopardy. Then, there had been nothing he could do. Here, there was still hope. He thought of that time. It had been a tragedy. His sister kidnapped. It had ended well. His sister was safe and completing her studies in the United States. Tara had intentions of joining Nassar Security in a full-time position when she graduated with her master's. He wasn't sure if he or any of his brothers were ready for that. He smiled at the thought, and his smile dropped as he looked at Ava. He pulled the blanket up, tucking it beneath her shoulders.

"How much longer, Jer?" he asked, although he already had the answer to that question. They were just words to fill the space, to make everything seem more normal.

"We're ten minutes out. How is she?"

"Unconscious," he said curtly. Nothing could make this normal and there was nothing more to say. Only Ava's thin breaths and her fragile pulse assured him that she was alive, that she was fighting to stay alive.

He had done all he could. The rest was up to Jer to get them onto the hospital helipad and Ava into medical experts' hands without delay.

"I've got this beauty flying her heart out," Jer assured him as if he'd read his mind. "We're only a few miles out now. She hanging in?"

"She's stable. Her breathing has leveled out. Pulse stable but a little faster than I'd like." He didn't like the way things were. For the truth was she hadn't regained consciousness in over ten minutes. Ahead, he could see the horizon open up on Miami. The city skyline appeared on the horizon and soon seemed to rise out of the ocean. Seagulls skimmed between sky and ocean. The slim stretch of sand became a dividing line between the endless stretch of ocean and the steel-and-glass high-rises that pierced the sky. The high-rises gleamed in the sun, which had broken through half an hour ago. The expanse of steel and glass set as a backdrop to the timeless ocean was postcard material. But now he could only allow for seconds of appreciation. They would be landing soon. It was noon and it seemed like they'd been at sea for days rather than hours. But the thought that medical help was now within sight had him breathing a sigh of relief. Ava had been unconscious for almost the entire trip. Faisal couldn't have imagined this day during the fun party days they'd shared. When they'd danced on the edges of a friendship that might have been more. In a way they'd been a platonic couple with the suggestion of more, and yet, they'd never crossed that line. It was strange, because the spark had been there. But he'd had another girlfriend at the time and even though that girl hadn't been the love of his life, it wasn't in him to cheat on one woman for another. Things might have been different otherwise. Why he thought of all that now, he didn't know.

He'd finally broken it off with his girlfriend at the time but Ava was too immersed in her studies to see the truth of what he felt. And he'd never asked her out or admitted that he felt so much more. He knew now that saying nothing was a youthful mistake. But time and life had intervened. He was reminded of it all now and faced with how much he still cared.

He looked out the window and below the city seemed to have taken over the landscape. One minute they were on the edge of the city and the next they were targeting a landing strip on the back edge of the hospital. A stretcher and an emergency team were already waiting.

The landing was smooth. The hospital staff were as efficient as the last time they had done this over a year ago; only this time, the roof helipad was closed for repairs and they were forced to divert to the original pad at ground level located just outside the emergency entrance.

On the ground there was a bit of chaos as reporters and camera operators pushed forward. They'd arrived as the stretcher was coming off the helicopter and the camera operators were in their faces almost immediately. They seemed to know who Ava was and more importantly who her father was. As Faisal forcibly pushed back against the onslaught, cameras flashed.

"Do you know where Dan Adams is?" a reporter asked, pushing the mic in his face.

Faisal ignored him, trying to shield the stretcher and Ava with his body.

"Is his daughter, Ava, the only survivor? What happened to Dan Adams? Has he been found?"

The questions were rapid-fire and Faisal had to push forward, demanding that they move back and give the stretcher room. It was the first sign of how much local fame Dan's philanthropy with local boys' and girls' clubs and other charities had given him. Dan had started an organization that reached out to troubled children, and it had branches across Florida and the Caribbean, where he lived for most of the year. His celebrity status put a different spin on this investigation too. Dan by himself was highly regarded, but with the power of his philanthropy, he was a force that couldn't go unacknowledged. They weren't points Faisal had time to consider; instead he was hauling an in-your-face cameraman back by the collar.

"Move back, please. Miss Adams is unable to answer your questions right now."

"Dan Adams?" The questions continued back-to-back. "Is there any hope?"

"The search is continuing," Faisal said.

Frustrating minutes passed before the media finally moved back. They hadn't gotten the information they came for but it was clear that it was the best they were going to get.

As the media moved away and the medical professionals took charge of the stretcher, there was nothing more for Faisal to do. He stood there, his hands shoved in his back pockets as he remembered Dan Adams's words in what might have been their last phone conversation. "I need your help, Faisal. I may have a case for you. The likes of which, I don't know if you've ever seen."

He wished he'd questioned him more, but at the time he'd thought it better to meet face-to-face. He'd looked forward to hearing what their old friend had been up to since they'd last been in touch and he'd even imagined how that meeting would go.

He moved through the bustling medics and to the stretcher that Ava had been transferred to. Her pallid complexion looked almost waxen like a model in a museum. Yet somewhere behind that beautiful still face lay answers. Whether what she might know included the answers they needed to find her father remained to be seen.

What had happened on that yacht off the coast of the Bahamas? From the little Ava had said, it had been deadly. The danger lay in whether or not the events that had caused Ava to end up looking death in the eye in a rubber raft would follow her. He could only hope that the danger had died on that yacht. But assumptions were never safe and too often proved to be wrong. He couldn't live his life on assumptions; if he did he would have been dead long ago. Her father was still out there and he needed to be found, for him—for Ava. His knuckle skimmed her soft cheek, remembering better times, and his right hand went to the butt of his gun. He wasn't taking any chances.

Chapter Seven

Ava entered the hospital on a stretcher led by a physician and with an assortment of other medical personnel flanking her. Faisal felt a sense of relief and panic all at the same time. They were feelings that he'd had from the beginning of this mysterious rescue. He should be relieved that she was in professional hands yet he also felt a profound sense of loss that she was out of his. He strode down the gleaming corridor. He made his way past bustling nurses and doctors and other medical personnel moving quickly through the corridors. He wondered what had brought Ava and her father to this. What had they been doing on that yacht? And where was Dan Adams?

He knew none of it boded well. The United States Coast Guard were coordinating efforts alongside the Bahama Search and Rescue. So far, Ava was the only survivor. There was no sign of the boat or Dan Adams.

He strode through the hospital's doors as he followed the stretcher that carried Ava as if somehow keeping her in his sights would keep her safe.

"Mr. Al-Nassar," a nurse called. "A minute, please."

At first, he didn't slow his stride. He wasn't used to being called by such a formal name. The only thing more formal would have been if they'd used his real title of Sheik. Again, something he never used. It was a title that was more accurate than mister, for, like his father before him and his grandfather before that, he was born a Sheik. But none of that was him. He was just Faisal Al-Nassar to everyone he knew and everyone he dealt with. No one in the Wyoming office called him by any title. They called him by his first name. Here, it was obviously different.

"Yes," he said, turning around despite his thoughts on the formality of the address, the hesitation being so slight as to be unnoticeable.

"There's some paperwork that needs to be completed."

"I'm not her next of kin," he said shortly.

The stretcher carrying Ava had now disappeared behind the sterile-looking stainless-steel doors ahead of him.

"You're the best we have at the moment," the nurse replied. "If we're lucky she may come to long enough to sign consent herself. But in the meantime, if you could just give us what you know."

He took the clipboard and the pen she offered and filled out the forms as best he could. There were large gaps in the information he provided. He knew nothing of her medical history or, barring Dan Adams, who her next of kin might be. He couldn't tell them if she were allergic to peanuts or anchovies or neither. He knew her stepfather, Dan, because he was a friend of the family. He knew that her birth father had died when she was a toddler. When her mother had married Dan, he had acquired a ten-year-old daughter. Unfortunately, Ava's mother had succumbed to a debilitating disease and died a decade ago. Dan and Ava were close. As close as any family he'd seen, even without the blood tie. Dan had taken parenting seriously and Ava was his daughter in the full meaning of that word. He handed the clipboard back to the nurse. Most of what he knew would be of no use to the medical team working on Ava.

He went to security next, explained the situation and ensured that she had a private room with a guard on the floor. Next, he went up to the floor and spoke to the nurses' station, ensuring that media were not allowed near her. He wasn't sure the latter was enough. He knew how tenacious media could be, especially when they sensed there was a story.

"Of course," the charge nurse replied. "She's not the first. We've had other local celebrities."

He wasn't sure how Ava would feel about being called a local celebrity. There was a bit of a mix-up in that, for it wasn't she who was the celebrity but her father. For Ava, he knew the media's interest would be bothersome. She'd always been very private. To him, that explained why she'd taken a position as a psychologist with a public school in Wyoming. The pace was quieter but more important, it was far away from her father's success and the notoriety that came with it. She was low-key. He'd always loved that about her.

Five minutes later he was exiting the hospital. She was in professional hands. Hands that had assured him that she would be well taken care of. In fact, they'd made it clear that there would be no visitors until she was stable. He'd gone over the contact information with a hospital administrator who had assured him that he would be notified as soon as there was a change. He gave the information, knowing that it was unnecessary. Barring the worst-case scenario, he'd be in touch long before any of them needed to reach him. In the meantime, her father, Dan Adams, his mentor, was still missing.

But his mind was stuck on other words. *Worst-case scenario.* There would be no worst-case scenario. He would not allow that to happen. Despite the fact that they'd fished Ava out of the Atlantic on a mission that could have easily failed. Despite the fact that the odds were still stacked against them, he was determined that those odds could be beaten. They would find out what happened. Otherwise he would have failed because now it was her father and an entire yacht that were missing.

Outside, with the Florida sun beating down on him, Faisal looked at the phone in his hand. The one that had been found with Ava. It was white, a basic, no-frills model, reminding him that Ava had learned her low-key approach to life from her father. She'd always been too busy getting good grades to put much thought into lip gloss or fashion. She'd been, at least then, a basics-only kind of girl. But despite that, there'd always been a sexy kind of appeal about her. Another year of maturity under her belt and he could have fallen for her. And yet that wasn't quite true—he'd wanted her even then, but the timing had been off. They were unproductive thoughts that weren't relevant to the situation. All of that was a long time ago and none of it mattered any longer.

He turned the phone over, but it provided no answers. He moved off the sidewalk, out of the way of a man in olive-toned hospital scrubs, moving briskly toward the parking lot.

"Barb," he said into his own phone a minute later. A light breeze wrapped around him and gently rustled the leaves of a nearby tree. He'd just phoned Barb Almay who headed Nassar's research team. She was located in their Marrakech office where she provided research for both Nassar offices. He explained the situation to her and then asked, "Can you run a check on this number's call activity?"

"Of course," Barb replied. She was their head researcher and a technical whiz almost on par with Craig. Their team was good but as far as researching went, Barb was the best—hands down. Barb was originally from Boston and had been on vacation in Morocco over a decade ago when she'd met a Moroccan man and fallen in love. The story had a fairy-tale ending—they'd married and she'd stayed in Morocco. Now she called Morocco home and it was there where she had been discovered by his brother Emir, and hired as part of the Nassar team.

He slipped the phone into his pocket and moved from beneath the shelter of the palm fronds. Overhead it was a clear sky and a seagull dipped and soared as if there was nothing wrong in the world. It sent a chill through him as he thought of the woman he'd left behind, unconscious, to the care of experts. He thought of the man still lost somewhere on the Atlantic and it was all incomprehensible.

His phone buzzed. It was Mitch Brandt, a man he'd gotten to know in his initial search-and-rescue training when he'd been fresh out of university and still debating whether a career with the Coast Guard might be an option. In the end he'd finished the initial training only out of interest, when the chance to head a new branch of Nassar had been presented to him. Mitch had completed the training and eventually gone to work with the US Coast Guard. Mitch had promised to keep him as up-to-date on the search as he could. They were conducting the search from where the yacht had last been seen off the coast of Paradise Island and beyond into the Atlantic Ocean. Yet the oddity they had found, Mitch said, hadn't been on water but on land.

When Faisal hung up, a frown creased between his brows. Only yesterday evening, shortly after dark on Paradise Island, a local had reported an incident regarding a strange man hiring a fisherman to take him to a yacht that had anchored a mile from shore. The incident had been unremarkable until the news of the

missing yacht had been leaked. They now knew that
the yacht had belonged to Dan Adams. There had been
two people on board. Dan Adams and his daughter,
Ava Adams. The description of the mystery man indicated only that he was of average height, forty to
sixty years old and Caucasian. A twenty-year age gap
left a lot of room for guessing.

Two knowns and an unknown on board who, except for Ava, had since disappeared. She had been rescued and the other two had vanished along with the
yacht. It was like something out of *The Twilight Zone*.
He strode back to the helipad where Jer and Sam were
waiting by the helicopter.

"What now?" Jer asked.

"You have to ask?" The question was redundant.
The thought that they wouldn't take at least one more
run wasn't even a consideration.

"I'm in," Sam said in that quiet, steady tone of his.

Thirty minutes later they were heading back out
to sea, where they searched until just after dark. But
there was nothing to be found. By mutual agreement
and before exhaustion set in, they called it a day. Faisal
sent an alert to the volunteer team coordinator to let
him know the area they'd been assigned on their second pass was searched and empty.

"I can't believe Dan's still out there," Faisal said.
"That we didn't find him."

"Not just him. There's the man with no name, as
well," Jer said. "Guy shows up and a few hours later
the yacht and its occupants go missing. Is there some

kind of link between the two events? Seems rather coincidental otherwise."

Faisal shook his head. He'd filled Jer in on the basics of the case, the search aspect anyway. "I don't know what that was about. Hopefully, Ava will be able to tell me something soon."

The lights of Miami's skyline lit the horizon. It was just short of nine o'clock in the evening. Faisal felt torn. He didn't want to end the search with Dan still out there but his heart was already back at Mercy Hospital afraid for Ava. Dan had an army of people looking for him; Ava had only him, or at least that's how it felt.

He pulled out his phone and placed a call. A minute later, he said, "Drop me at the hospital. The helipad is clear and there aren't any emergencies coming in." He'd just checked with the hospital authorities and, considering the circumstances, they were okay with a quick drop and leave. "You get home to your wife."

"She's not too happy with you," Jer said with a smile. He'd called earlier to let his wife know what was up.

"Doesn't matter what she thinks of me," Faisal said with a laugh. "She loves you, man. That's why you get away with murder. But you've made her wait long enough."

They'd already discussed the fact that Jer had commitments at home in Tampa. He had a wife and kids waiting for him and while his plans could and would be broken if Faisal asked—that wouldn't happen. Jer was a contract worker that he'd used often. He was also one of the best heli-pilots he knew. When this had all come down, he'd taken advantage of the resources he'd had in the moment. He'd contacted Jer only because they'd worked rescue before and Florida was his home state.

Sam, like Jer, had worked with him before on other cases and they were both based out of Miami. The rest of it, the fact that Craig was heading to the east coast anyway, had been a stroke of good luck. He'd known that if anyone could find out where that phone signal had come from and get to it in time, he could. He'd been right in thinking that and in doing what he had. He'd cobbled together the powerhouse team in minutes after hearing the news. They'd done what they'd set out to do. Now, there were search-and-rescue teams combing the area from both countries. But there was still no sign of the yacht or Dan Adams. He could only hope that he was still onboard, for then he stood a chance.

It was because of everything Dan had done for him and everything he'd been that Faisal had left Ava's side for the length of time he had. But if her father's life depended on it, he couldn't do otherwise.

"What's next?" Jer asked. The helicopter had just landed.

"I'm having a check run on the phone we found with Ava," Faisal replied.

"We're not heading back out?" Despite their earlier agreement, Jer sounded oddly disappointed. "I've got the rest of the night, man, if you need me."

"And Rene," he said, referring to Jer's wife, "will blame me when you don't come home at all tonight." He was fully capable of flying one of the company planes or helicopters if it came to that. "I'm going to wait. We've been out twice—had success once. Now I want to make sure Ava's alright."

"There's nothing you can do if she isn't," Jer said.

"True. But I don't like leaving her alone."

They were silent as a Jeep pulled into the adjoining parking lot.

"That's my ride," Sam said and a minute later he was departing with a nod.

"You knew her in college, didn't you?" Jer asked after Sam left, raising the subject with a worried look at Faisal.

"Yeah, we were friends. Her father and she were always considered family friends, no matter that I lost touch with Ava." The thought of how close they'd been and how easily it all came back at the sight of her was disquieting. "I'm hoping that Ava knows something. They've all the manpower they can muster on the search," he said, looking toward the Atlantic. "We've given it our all. Time for a rest. You might as well go home. You're supposed to be on vacation."

"Yeah, right." Jer grinned. "Rene has a list of odd jobs for me to do. More than I could get done in three weeks never mind six days." He shrugged. "Some vacation. In the meantime, I better get this bird home," he said, referring to the helicopter.

After Jer had left, Faisal received a call from Barb in their Marrakech office.

"I don't have a lot," she said. "But I thought you might want what I do have, for now anyway."

If the situation hadn't been so dire Faisal might have smiled. Barb often qualified her research as less than what she actually had. He waited for her to prove him right. "Let me have what you know," he said.

"As you know, the phone belonged to Dan Adams. That particular phone was on a pay-as-you-go plan. There wasn't anything unusual about any of it. What was intriguing though were the number of calls received from Vancouver. Over half dozen within three days."

"Vancouver, Washington?"

"British Columbia, Canada," she said. "I used some tech to unmask the private phone numbers and, as always, it worked like a dream. Interesting fact… a few actually—I don't have a name to go with the number, but I managed to get a location. Those calls were made from a Vancouver number in an area that, well, let's just say it's *very* wealthy. Many who live there are first-generation immigrants from China." She paused as if considering this seriously important. "So far that's all I have. I'm still working on the name of the caller."

He thanked her and ended the call shortly after that. As he hung up, he thought of everything that had transpired in recent days. Only three hours ago, in Fort Lauderdale, he was to have met with Dan. That hadn't happened. Now it might never happen. Fate had intervened in a particularly grim way. She had a harsh sense of humor, one he'd never much appreciated. He pushed that thought aside.

For now, they had nothing but tragedy on their hands.

Faisal clenched his fist. He'd lost too many people he cared about. He refused to let anything further happen to Ava and he prayed they found Dan.

But the facts weren't encouraging. And until either the yacht or Dan Adams was found, the only witness he had was an unconscious woman. His instinct told him that the answer to all this lay on that yacht. But the Atlantic was a big place to get lost in.

Chapter Eight

"Log the case as a code orange," Faisal said as he reported in for the second time to the home office in Jackson, Wyoming. Nassar coded all its cases in four categories from white to red. White was no threat to the investigator. Red was the most dangerous to client and investigator. Orange was the second highest rating. It meant that there was the possibility of danger to the investigator and an obvious threat to the client.

The whole case stunk. He didn't like the sound of the man who had arrived uninvited on the yacht just hours before tragedy struck. It was all too convenient, even easy, and that always spelled trouble. If it smelled like trouble—it was trouble.

He thought of their research team already working overtime and thought of how he'd be dead in the water without them. On both sides of the Atlantic, Marrakech and Jackson, Wyoming, their research and admin teams were the best. In fact, in the past, they'd had other companies try to lure some of their researchers away. The attempts had been unsuccessful. The benefits that Nassar offered its employees were unmatched, but then money had never been an issue for his family. He and his three brothers and sister had been born into wealth. Despite generous donations to charity, they became wealthier with each passing year.

At twenty-seven, Faisal was a wealthy man. It wasn't something he gave much consideration to, it just was. He had an accountant and an investing team who handled such things. He made sure his employees were well compensated. That was Nassar company policy. Their employees worked hard and without them, he knew his success wouldn't have come as easily or as quickly. That aside, with trusted employees in place, Faisal could stick to what he was good at and what he loved. He loved what he did—at work and at play. He played hard and he worked hard. Now, despite plans earlier in the week to learn to surf in Florida after his meeting with Dan followed by a snowboarding trip, he was back at work. It was clear that this case, wherever it was going to take him, was going to take some time.

His phone buzzed. He picked up before it had a chance to alert him twice.

"What's going on, Fai?" his brother Talib asked.

"Ava's been in and out of consciousness. But at least she's safe and being taken care of. She'll make it," Faisal said. After the almost six months that Talib had been in Wyoming, Faisal now wondered how he had functioned without him. Zafir had always shared his time between Marrakech and Wyoming. "There's no sign of the yacht. There are search teams out there now. Jer, Sam and I just got in from searching, although we brought Ava in early this afternoon." While he'd given a formal account to the office, he always liked to speak personally to his brother, if he happened to be in the office.

"Any word yet on Dan Adams?" Talib asked with concern in his voice.

"Nothing," Faisal said. "Nothing's adding up on this, T," he said. His middle brother, Talib had only recently relocated to Wyoming to raise his son, Everett, with his new wife, Sara. Talib was now his backup and had taken the helm as cohead. For Faisal, it had been a relief to have the pressure of being in charge eased. Unlike his other brothers, he would rather have more free time than more power and the responsibility that came with it. He and Talib were similar in that way. He believed that was because his mother had placed less restrictions on them as children and had insisted that a day was lost without a bit of fun. It was a concept he'd carried into adulthood. A jolt of sadness ran through him at the thought of her. He'd lost both his parents years ago in a tragic accident that only recently had been found to have a murderous twist. A case his eldest brother, Emir, had taken on had been the one that revealed the new information, which had threatened to destroy the family. But they'd made it through and their family had grown and become stronger. Now it was up to him to make someone else's family whole again.

"Dan Adams wasn't alone. Another passenger, an unidentified middle-aged male, as well as the yacht they were on, seem to have disappeared. There's no more information than that. Ava is our only witness and according to her attending physician, she's suffering traumatic memory loss. She was in bad shape when she came in. They did a preliminary assessment before I left. When I called a few minutes ago, I was told that physically she's coming around quickly but her memory is still not there. The Bahama Search and Rescue confirms the presence of another man—he was sighted by a local but they have no name."

"Wait a minute," Talib interrupted. "Zafir wants to speak to you."

A minute later his second eldest brother, and Emir's twin, was on the line. Zafir was vice president of the company and floated between the two offices.

"Do you need me there?" he asked. "I'm at loose ends before I fly home. I'll be back in Marrakech at the end of the week. Unless, of course, you're in desperate need of a hand."

"Not now. I'll let you know if this thing catches fire. Otherwise, I'll keep at it on my own. The United States Coast Guard and the Bahamas Air Sea Rescue and a bevy of other volunteers are out there. More volunteers than I've ever seen on a sea rescue."

"Alright," Zafir agreed. "The other agents are all

working on cases and, as you know, Talib was just assigned one. But I'm all yours if you need me. For now."

For now.

They were words that they lived by, for circumstances in their business could change in an instant. And something in his gut told him that this one was about to do just that.

Five minutes later Faisal shook his head as he disconnected from his contact within the Coast Guard. There was no information since they'd last spoken. It seemed the only thing they'd been able to prove was what they already knew. The Adamses' yacht had disappeared without a trace. It was as if only Ava and the life raft they'd found her in remained as evidence that the yacht had ever existed.

It was just after ten o'clock in the evening when Faisal returned to the hospital. In his earlier phone call to check on Ava's status, he'd learned that she was going for a CAT scan. He was advised to wait a few hours until that and a variety of other tests were completed. Despite the leads he'd followed in the interim, he'd chaffed at not being able to see Ava sooner. But the physician he'd spoken to had encouraged him to give her some time. She'd been "through a trauma" were the physician's exact words and she needed a few hours of quiet and rest.

Anxious to see her, he took the stairs instead of waiting for the elevator. Even when he wasn't on a case and in a rush, he preferred stairs since he found elevators closed-in and claustrophobic. Besides that, the whole process, even with the latest and most swift of elevators, was still slowed down by the time it took humans to load and unload. He had no patience for that and so, as he usually did, took the stairs. He ran the six flights and arrived just as the elevator doors opened and a trio of medical personnel entered the floor.

At the desk, he stopped and waited as a pretty brunette finished a phone call before looking at him with a question in her eyes.

"I'm here to see Ava Adams," he said.

"Room 610," she said as if he needed that information.

"Is the attending physician available?" he asked. "I have a few questions." The physician he'd spoken to earlier had not been her attending.

Five minutes later he was striding down the hall, his expression grim. What he'd heard hadn't boded well. She was fragile, awake and alert, if you could call still having no memory alert. She was on a secure floor in a private room, as he'd insisted. He'd thought that her youth and the vibrancy that he remembered would have her healing faster than what the physician said was normal progress. Nothing about Ava was normal. Despite what he was told, he had high hopes that she'd be able to fill in the many blanks.

"Ava," Faisal said as he leaned over the standard hospital bed's security railing. An intravenous machine beeped as it filtered medication into a line in her left hand.

She looked at him at first with puzzlement as if she didn't know where she was or who he might be. Disappointment coursed through him. If she didn't remember him, then what were the chances she was able to remember anything about what had happened aboard that yacht? Yet it was the former that bothered him. He'd never forgotten her and now it appeared she'd completely forgotten not only him but everything else in her life. The case slipped momentarily to the background.

"It's me… Faisal," he said as if maybe he'd read the expression on her face wrong, as if maybe there was still hope.

She didn't say anything and the hope slipped from his heart.

She didn't know him. He could see that there was no recognition in her eyes. He hadn't expected that. Somehow, he had hoped that under medical care she would have bounced back. Despite what he knew and what the physician had told him, he'd held to that belief.

"Faisal Al-Nassar," he said as if he were approaching a stranger. And despite his formality all he wanted to do was comfort her, hold her and tell her that she was safe.

"Faisal," she murmured but there was no recognition in her eyes.

"We were friends," he said hating the past tense. He sucked back disappointment. They were friends now, at least he wanted them to be. Disappointment coursed through him. He'd imagined that she'd greet him with that lazy smile of hers and offer him a second chance, that he'd again be her everything. He mentally stepped back at the thought. Where had that come from? The thought had been as unexpected as the desire behind it. He'd never been her everything. Given a second chance with Ava, he'd take it. But they'd danced so far from that to where they were now, and back then they'd been only friends. She didn't remember him, the intimacy they'd shared, the intuitive knowing— all of that was gone. They'd both went their separate ways. But the truth was he'd never forgotten her. And now that she was back in his life, he wasn't planning to lose her again.

His thoughts were totally selfish. She'd been through hell and he was expecting her to react to his presence like she had a long time ago. That was the past. He needed to forget about what they had been, who they had been and deal with the now, the present. He was being insensitive, as his sister, Tara, would accuse him. But she was the member of the family who kept everyone in line. The only girl, she was his closest sibling and the family's heart.

"Where's my father?" Ava whispered, breaking into his thoughts and reminding him that he wasn't the only one with family. Her family was missing.

Where was Dan Adams? It was the question that brought him back to reality, back to what was important. It was the question that was the crux of this case. Her words reminded him that there were more important things that needed addressing than old feelings between the two of them. He couldn't believe he'd even allowed those thoughts any purchase at a time like this. Did she know he was missing? How could she?

"You were the last person who saw him." He wanted to add the word *alive*. It was on the tip of his tongue but its shock value would do neither of them any good. "Is there anything you remember? Anything that might help us locate him?"

"Is he alright?" She struggled to sit up. The look on her face was pained.

He regretted bringing that look of pain to her. She'd had enough trauma and now he'd only added more.

"I don't remember," she said as she fell back onto the bed. She shook her head. "I can't remember." She clenched the sheet and again struggled to sit up.

"No." He placed a hand on her shoulder. "You need to rest. You've had a trauma, a shock. You were unconscious, you…"

"My father," she bit out. "We have to find him before he kills him."

Shock at her words rippled through him. She'd said the words earlier when they'd first rescued her. Somehow then they were less shocking, more easily placed into the context of her situation—perhaps even a hallucination. He could hear the fear in her voice.

Faisal frowned. "Who wants to kill whom?"

"I don't know," she said. "I can't remember. I just know that when he finds him…" The words trailed off as though she'd lost the energy to continue. She bit her lip, chewing on it before relaxing, but her eyes narrowed. It was clear that she believed every word she had said. "He's going to kill him."

She shook her head. Tears glistened and threatened to spill over.

She looked away, her hand clutching the bed rail and her heart monitor sped up.

"Ava?"

He wanted to take her in his arms. He wanted to make all of this go away and he could do neither of those things. He thought of the man with no name who had joined Dan Adams and Ava that fateful night. Who was he? Was he a threat to Dan? To Ava? Was it possible that he had something to do with the yacht going missing? There were too many possibilities that only seemed to increase every time he went through the questions. He hated to do this to her but she had been there. She knew. If she could only remember. "What happened, Ava?"

She looked at him, really looked at him, like she had in the past. Like she had when they'd danced together and laughed like friends and, he'd never admitted it to himself or to her but, he'd wanted so much more. That was half a decade ago—a lifetime. She shook her head and closed her eyes.

She was fading.

He ran a finger along her forehead, brushing back her dark hair. Her skin was damp. There were dark shadows beneath her closed eyes. She needed rest and she didn't need him haranguing her for answers. He was afraid to leave her alone and yet afraid to not be part of the search. He knew from the physician's report that she slept in short spurts and was awake at odd hours through the day. He sat with her the remainder of the night and she seemed to settle down as she slept through the night. This time it was he who slept off and on, watching her every moment he was awake.

He'd been on the go almost twenty-four hours, watching her, keeping her safe while he catnapped— this was his break.

In the early hours of the morning, he reluctantly decided to start his day. The hospital was beginning to come to life. He stopped at the nurses' station on the way out. There he was told that Ava had another lineup of tests that day. He knew she was in good hands at the moment. The search for her father was more in need of his efforts. Ava was safe. Her father was not. So he went out with one of the volunteer pilots that morning and through the afternoon. They searched an area the Coast Guard considered important. But bad weather, the yacht's failed equipment or the chance that the vessel had drifted far away from shipping lines could keep the craft off the radar. Despite the efforts of the United States Coast Guard, the Bahamas Air Sea Rescue Association and numerous other volunteers, there was still no sign of the missing yacht.

DAN ADAMS HAD been in and out of consciousness. There was one constant. Always the wet, hard surface

pressed against his face. Sometimes the screech of a
bird but more often the slap of waves against the bow
awoke him. This time when he woke up the pain in
his head and the light were blinding. He knew who
he was but he wasn't sure where he was. That aside,
he could only think of one person, his daughter, Ava.
He remembered getting her in the raft. He remembered it swinging clear of the yacht. He even remembered it hitting the water. It was the gunshot that had
thrown him backward. Now, his shoulder ached but
the bleeding had stopped. He'd been grazed. When
the bullet had hit him, he'd been thrown into the
water. After the initial impact, he had struggled and
trod water before he'd finally managed to pull himself up and onto the yacht by sheer will. He wasn't
going to die, not with Ben still alive, a threat to his
daughter. He remembered nothing after those traumatic moments.

Now, his mind was filled with worry for Ava. Was
she alright? Had Ben gotten her too? For it was clear in
his short periods of wakefulness that Ben had left him
for dead, dead and adrift at sea. He wasn't sure but he
didn't think that there was anyone else on the yacht.

"Av..." What should have been his daughter's name
came out no more than a choked cough. It was strange,
for one moment he knew she wasn't there and the next
moment he thought she was, or maybe he just hoped.
He couldn't speak, he could barely breathe and he was
fighting to live. He turned on his side and coughed.
Blood mixed with spit and sea water ran in a faded

stream down the deck. He tried to sit up but his head spun and his ribs ached so badly he thought he would vomit again. He imagined his ribs were broken. It wasn't an improbable thought, for every breath was too painful to contemplate. Moving was impossible, he could barely tolerate the simple act of breathing. His head felt like it had been split open and as he slowly dragged his hand out from under his body and felt the side of his head, he could feel something warm trickling down his face. Blood.

His thoughts were cloudy and he shivered. The breeze off the ocean was cool and it seemed to chill his already damp skin. He tried to get to his feet once but his legs shook so hard that he lost his balance and crashed to the deck. But he'd been on his feet long enough to see that at least on the deck, he was alone, and around him there was nothing—only water.

Hours passed or it might have only been minutes.

He didn't know where he was or how long he'd been there.

Finally, he pulled himself off the deck, supporting himself on one knee, both legs too shaky to stand up completely. It had been hours, days even since he'd eaten or had any water. He needed to hydrate at the least so that he could live, for if he didn't Ben would kill Ava. If he hadn't already.

He reached for his phone.

Gone.

He remembered leaving it with Ava.

A feeling of dread snaked down his spine. He

could only hope that Ava had contacted Faisal Al-Nassar. That hope was all that now stood between them and death.

Chapter Nine

Sunday, June 12—8:00 a.m.

Faisal strode toward Ava's hospital bed. He was relieved to see that, as the physician had just assured
him, she was much better than the day before. Last
night, when he'd sat with her, he'd been unable to tell
anything of her alertness or change in status, for she'd
slept through the night. His being there now seemed
like it may have been more for him than her. He'd
needed to know she was alright.

Now it was clearly different. She was awake and he
could see that some of the vibrancy he remembered
had returned. Her eyes had life to them and there was
color in her cheeks. He smiled back at Ava as she gave
him a smile of recognition. It was a relief to see her
conscious and what appeared to be coherent. He came
forward with long strides and took her free hand between both of his.

Her dark hair gleamed under the fluorescent lights.

Her eyes shone with welcome despite the pallor of her skin and the beeping of machines that surrounded her.

"You're looking better than I expected," Faisal said. He let go of her hand and took a step back, not wanting to overwhelm her. At the same time, he realized that what he'd just said was slightly, if not completely, insulting. It wasn't what he had meant to say, not at all. But considering the circumstances he thought he might be forgiven. After all, he had saved her life. Unfortunately, he'd yet to save her father's. They weren't even sure that there was anything to save. That thought took any levity he might have felt at seeing Ava better completely away. "At least, better than yesterday," he added as if that made his faux pas any better.

Ava was sitting half up, propped by two pillows. And her smile was a surprise, considering what he'd said and how he'd said it. But then she hadn't been privy to his thoughts. And looking at her he doubted whether she had the strength to come back at him the way she used to. They had enjoyed their verbal sparring during their friendship. He was reminded again of how quick she had been, now that there was no answering repartee. It was unfair even as a thought, for he knew that she was in no shape for such things. She was physically fragile but still as gorgeous as ever. Her face was slimmer, her cheekbones more defined and her lips as they'd always been, full and naturally red.

He met the look of concern in her eyes that begged him for answers. But he didn't have any, not yet. And he had to quit thinking about how beautiful she was, how lush her figure was even in the hospital attire. Instead, he gave her a slight smile. "How are you feeling?"

This time, she smiled wanly as if sitting partway up with her head supported by pillows was almost too much for her. Beside her, the intravenous machine quietly beeped. He'd spoken to her physician, who had assured him that it was only a matter of getting her hydrated and then the intravenous would be discontinued. And at the speed she'd been recovering in the last few hours, she'd be ready for discharge in a day or two, at most.

"Fai," she said, her voice thin as she spoke in a whisper. There was a hoarse edge to the word, as if her throat was still raw from her experience. "I haven't seen you in a long time. Too long."

It was like yesterday and the day before had never existed. It was like she perceived everything in a different way than how it had happened. "The nurse said you saved me." The words were weak as if it was all she could do to get them out. She closed her eyes again, as if the light hurt or maybe the effort of keeping them open was just too much.

"I got you off the life raft, anyway," he said in a lighthearted way. He didn't want to act like the heavy, not in her state. Besides, this was the first true conversation they'd had since he'd rescued her.

She opened her eyes and smiled at him. "That's all?" she asked and her words were so quiet he almost didn't hear them. Yet there was an edge in her tone. Something that, this time, reminded him of the Ava he had known—quick-witted, sharp, never letting anything slip by her.

"What do you mean?"

"Always modest, you saved my life," she said with another attempt at a smile, but the smile didn't reach her eyes. "Thank you doesn't quite cover it."

"No thanks necessary," he replied. He felt like they were stuck in some impersonal chat loop. Where neither wanted to admit that they had anything more intimate than a general knowledge of the other. He wanted to ask her so many questions but he didn't want to tire her. He needed to start with the most critical. Instead she beat him to it.

"Where's my father? I need to see him." Her breathing seemed to both speed up and become more shallow at the same time. Her heart monitor sped up slightly.

"Ava."

Somehow her name was a substitute for the answer he couldn't speak, at least not to her. It was too bleak. But before he could say anything more she had slipped farther back into the pillows and closed her eyes as if it was all too much. A minute passed and then two. She opened her eyes and seemed to connect with him for a second before she shut them again.

He looked away from her as if needing a reprieve from the power of that connection. Her gaze seemed to demand that he get the answers she needed. It was ridiculous really, but that had been the Ava he knew, determined, smart—stubborn. Even now, it was as if she hadn't been to hell and back, and it gave him hope that her memory would return soon. As it stood everything hinged on her memory. Without it, he could have no idea how she had ended up in a dinghy alone in the middle of the Atlantic or who might be left on that boat. It was all a mystery.

He turned back. There was a shimmer of tears in her eyes and she clenched the sheet.

"Anything you can remember, Ava? The smallest bit of information could be helpful. I know things may be a little gray right now but your memory will return."

Silence lay heavy between them. A metal cart lumbered down the corridor and past her room. The noise was loud and grating.

He looked at his watch. It was large, oval faced with a black leather strap and a manual wind, a relic from another generation. He wound it as if just remembering the fact that time was slipping away and still they were not much further ahead. It was frustrating, especially when he guessed that much of what he needed to know was locked somewhere deep in Ava's mind. He put his hand over hers as if that would make everything better, as if somehow the contact would jog her memory.

"I have a watch like that," she said as if that was of paramount importance. "One that winds, I mean."

"I know," he said brushing his hand against the back of hers, feeling the soft skin and remembering other times. "I gave it to you."

Silence descended again. He waited, hoping for answers about that night, the night that mattered most. The night that had changed everything.

"I…" Ava whispered. She shivered as if the memories of that night, few as they were, were too much and too overwhelming.

He leaned closer.

The only thing they knew for sure was that there were three people on the yacht that night. Dan Adams, the registered owner; Ava; and the man who had arrived later. What had happened that evening? Had there been an altercation of some kind? What had been the catalyst for her to be in that life raft? Had her father been trying to save her from a sinking vessel or from something much more deadly?

Dan Adams might very well be the victim of foul play. But he had no evidence, and he'd yet to admit to Ava that her father was missing despite the fact that she'd asked. She was fragile right now and he didn't know what she knew or didn't know. All that aside, it was his job to protect her, physically, emotionally—the latter was impossible, he knew that but he'd do his best.

"Tell me, Ava, what do you remember?" He knew he was pushing but if Dan was still alive they could well be running out of time. He didn't offer her a hint of what little he knew. He only hoped that she could remember something of what had occurred between the time that she had ended up in a life raft and the yacht had disappeared.

"I wish I could tell you, Fai, but I just don't know." She shook her head. "I'm remembering the past." Her voice shook. "You—school, all of that. But what happened on Dad's yacht—nothing."

He nodded, expecting that, as he'd been warned by her physician, and fighting for patience when he knew that time was imperative.

He sat down on the chair by her bedside, preferring that to looming over her, which seemed to him to be slightly intimidating. He reached over and pushed a strand of hair from her cheek. Heat seemed to run up his arm at the brief contact and he pulled back as if he'd been burned.

"Fai," she murmured. Her free hand lifted as if reaching for him and then dropped. She shook her head. "I'm so sorry. I'm trying…"

"Don't rush it. It will come back," he assured her but he'd barely said that when her eyes widened.

"Ben…he was new. They did business together, he and my father. He was there. He wanted something. What it was, I don't know, or if I did, I don't remember. Dad had a lot of irons in the fire, as you know. He couldn't seem to stick to one business venture at a time. I think at one point he was even invested in a car dealership. And, of course he was successful at them all. Maybe that was the trouble," she said with a hint of irony.

"So Ben was on board?" He forced the excitement from his voice. Now they were getting somewhere.

"Yes," she said, surprise etching her voice. "Now

that you're talking about it, encouraging me to re-member I mean…" She looked at him with a rather wispy smile. "I remember that now. He wasn't ex-pected. At least I don't think he was. I met him once before, briefly. I remember that. He threatened…" She shook her head. "I'm not sure. I can't even remember his full name." It was the most she had yet to say and her voice was hoarse and barely audible by the time she got to the last words.

He was silent. There was little he could offer. Be-sides, outside opinion could change or even implant memories, somehow change her reality or how she perceived what had happened. He smiled, remember-ing her off-the-cuff psychology lessons all those years ago. He'd taken behavioral courses. But no course was as fascinating as seeing the passion in her eyes as she shared her enthusiasm for what made the human brain tick.

"Darrell Chan," she said unexpectedly.

"Who?" He leaned forward, the tension palpable. He knew that they were getting somewhere. "Was he on the yacht?"

She shook her head. "No."

"Who is he? How do you know him?" *Too many questions*, he chastised himself. He was threatening to overwhelm her and yet time had never seemed so tight.

She shook her head. Her lips were taut and her face was almost devoid of color. "I don't know."

Yet she'd given him the name as if it were the key to a national treasure. He looked at her. She was looking straight ahead as if she were deep in thought or more importantly, trying to capture her thoughts.

Two names. Two men. How did they fit together?

"Who are they?"

Again, she shook her head, her lips pinched.

"Do you know where either of them are from?" He hoped to at least narrow the names down geographically if nothing else.

She shook her head and began to look distressed. "Ben…" she murmured. "He had a gun," she said. Her voice was weak but determined. "And he said he'd kill him."

"Ben was there?"

"Yes."

"Was Darrell Chan there?" he asked. The repetition was only a precaution, a test on the blips of moments that she was remembering.

"No."

She shook her head.

"Ava," he whispered.

"Dad was going to report him," she whispered. "Ben," she said before he could ask. "He was so angry at my father."

Faisal leaned forward.

He stopped questioning her. She wasn't a prisoner and he'd almost begun an interrogation. He stood up, leaning over her and taking the hand that was free of the intravenous line between his. It felt soft and vulnerable against his skin. He thought of all she'd been through and tried with the small gesture to reassure her that he was on her side. That he was her friend and that… He killed the thought. There was no time to think of other things, of other longings, of other needs. And yet, in a delicate state of health or not, she still did things to him that no other woman could.

Ava was noticeably fading, her eyes were half-closed and her voice was trailing off.

Silence filled the room. Her eyes finally closed and her breathing was even. It was like she'd fallen asleep. He knew the pattern of this now. He waited, letting her gather her strength and, he imagined, weave together her fragmented thoughts.

Another minute. His patience was shredding and yet none of this was her fault. It was a ludicrous thought. The only thing he could give her was comfort and little of that, considering he couldn't bring back her father by his will alone.

"Ben," she whispered. "Whyte."

"Your father was going to report him?"

"Yes."

In the hallway, outside the closed door, another cart rattled past.

"Ben was there," she whispered. Her full lips chapped and pale. "That night…"

"On the yacht," he encouraged. It was information he already knew—at least he knew about the stranger. Now he had a name.

"Where is my dad and the yacht?"

He shook his head. He couldn't tell her this and

yet he couldn't lie. "I don't know, Ava. We're search-ing for him."

A tear slid down her cheek. He clasped her free hand tighter wanting to take the pain of what he'd told her away. She shuddered and turned her face away; the seconds ticked by, but when she turned to face him it was like her mind was elsewhere.

It was then that Ava said, "Phony land. Big trouble," and then she passed out.

They were bizarre words and a simplistic way of speaking that was not like Ava. It was as if she had taken a step backward after all her progress. But con-sidering the trauma she had been through he supposed it wasn't unusual. Still he worried. He sat by her side and wondered how it had all come to this. Her dark hair hung in lackluster tangles that framed her face. He arranged her pillow so that she was raised to the angle the physician had recommended.

The monitor began to beep a warning. Her blood pressure had just dropped. He hit the call bell and rolled her onto her side, propping her in that position with one of the pillows. It was one of many things he'd learned in his emergency medical training when he'd certified for sea rescue work. Before he could get to the door to shout for help, two nurses were in the room. They assured him that the physician was en route. He was directed to the hallway with an effi-ciency that would have impressed him at another time.

He hung back in the corridor until she was again stable. What was clear in the aftermath was that there would be no visitors of any kind for the next few hours. The attending physician had been adamant.

He could deal with that. There were things he needed to do now that she was safe once again. No thanks to him, he thought rather ironically—he believed that it had been his questions that had upset her and brought her close to another medical crisis.

He was left with the sure knowledge that time was running out.

"WHAT DO YOU HAVE?" Faisal asked as he answered his phone. He'd just left Ava's side and was about to put in a call with the new information when Barb's number showed as the incoming call. Barb didn't call unless she had something. She'd been with the company long enough that minor research was immediately dumped to one of five other employees. Interestingly enough, they were all women. He wasn't sure what that might mean, if anything.

"I have a name of someone else on Dan Adams's yacht that night. Ben Whyte," she said briskly. "It isn't much but I thought that I'd at least give you what I know so you have something to go on."

That was part of what made Barb great in the office. She was aware of the pieces that needed to link together to make a case work. She was always one step ahead of the investigators in the field, getting information to them quickly and efficiently. She'd unearthed the most difficult piece of evidence in record time.

"Ben Whyte was picked up on the beach of Paradise Island. The identity pickup was just good luck. Anyway, goes like this. The local fisherman who took him out said he dropped a driver's licence. State of Florida," she said before he could ask. "He found it later at the back of his boat but by the time he had a chance to return it, Ben was gone. He turned it in to the local authorities but it wasn't really of much interest until now."

"Ava just confirmed that he was on board. Interesting turn of events."

"So she's conscious?" Barb asked.

"Most of the time," he replied. "She said that a man named Ben Whyte joined them later." He remembered that she'd also said that it was unexpected. "If he's connected with Dan he may have spent some time in the Caribbean where Dan lives part of the year. Just a guess but…"

"I'll get what I can on this Whyte character," Barb said before he could ask. He could hear her clicking away and knew she was digging answers out of the internet. He waited. Sometimes she was so quick that there was no point ending the call, she would only end up calling back.

A minute passed and then two. He'd learned a lot in the field, working on so many cases that involved a mystery. Two of the things he'd learned were determination and patience.

"Several people by that name but only one who has recently been in the Caribbean," Barb said as if there had been no break in the conversation. "Not sure if there's any relevance, but he changed his name thirty-six years ago from Tominski to Whyte."

"No criminal record?"

"None that I can find. Not sure why the name change," Barb replied. "But I'll let you know what else I find. By the way, I'm still working on your Vancouver connection."

"Look into land transactions and also a man by the name of Darrell Chan. I know I just keep piling it on."

"I love the challenge," she laughed.

"That's good because there's more. I remember Adams talking about some land speculation. I didn't think anything of it. But then Ava said something that was odd. 'Phony land.'"

"Phony land?"

"I know, strange. And then she said big trouble."

"The mind works in mysterious ways, especially when it's been through a shock," Barb said.

"True," he agreed. "It's got to mean something. I know that Adams wanted to meet about land. In fact, he said that it was nothing he wanted to talk about over the phone."

"Interesting," Barb replied.

"Exactly," Faisal agreed. "See if there's anything recent, and then go back as far as you have to. Use all three names, Adams, Tominski and Whyte."

"Done," she replied. "And stay safe," Barb demanded. She had been with them for so long she was like family, watching out for each of them, worrying from the safety of the office.

"I will," he said, ending the call and thinking only of how his safety was secondary to finding Ava's father. He needed to find Dan Adams soon for he sensed that time was running out.

Chapter Ten

Sunday, June 12—9:30 p.m.

Ava took a deep breath as the nurse left her room. She had bounced back in the last few hours. She knew that from the way everything seemed clearer rather than a confusing cloud of sound. She also knew she was better by the fact that she didn't want to constantly sleep and, most telling of all, she was now remembering big chunks of previously forgotten events.

Faisal had been here again and just left. She admired and appreciated his dedication. Something came alive within her just knowing that he was near. But there was something she needed to do without him. He'd just left—that meant that he wouldn't be returning again for at least a few hours. She'd encouraged him to get some sleep but she knew that he would get the minimal necessary before returning to be with her. She'd demanded that he stay at the hotel and at least get a night's sleep. She'd finally gotten that promise out of him.

The machine on her left beeped but the one on her right was quiet. It was only a blood pressure machine, which the physician had just used, assuring her that her blood pressure was normal.

Ava was remembering things that she hadn't told Faisal, things she hadn't told anyone. Truthfully, she'd remembered none of it when he had asked. And if she had, she didn't know if she would have told him.

Faisal.

She'd once fancied herself in love with him. But she'd been young, what had she known about love or life or any of it for that matter? She pushed the thoughts away. The past didn't matter. She knew that she kept returning to it because it was the only clarity she had, that and a gut instinct that she had to get out of here. She also knew that she couldn't involve anyone else, for to do so would be to place them in danger. Even Faisal couldn't know what she planned, for despite what he did for a living, it didn't make him invulnerable. She needed to get out of here, alone. It was on her shoulders to put a stop to this. She didn't consider the irony that she didn't know what she needed to stop. All she knew was that if she didn't succeed both she and her father were in trouble. That is, if her father was still alive. The thought choked her and tears trembled on her lashes.

She shook her head. She couldn't think like that. She'd survived and her father would too. She clung to what she did know. One place and a memory that were branded in her mind. She didn't know what they meant. She only knew that she had to get to that place to find answers.

But her emotions were raw as she thought of the feel of her hand in Faisal's. Her heart felt like it stopped at the thought of him. He was gone. She hadn't seen him in five years but she'd thought of him often. She tore her thoughts from Faisal and to what she needed to remember. A tremor ran through her. Her father. The last time she'd seen him was when she'd been in the life raft. She remembered a feeling of panic of wanting to reach out and help. He'd been on the yacht and then she'd lost sight of him and remembered only the feeling of horror and helplessness that had enveloped her. Where was he now?

She could remember that the doctor had told her that her memory would come back. She remembered studying about memory. She remembered studying a lot of things. What she didn't remember were the last hours on her father's yacht and they were the most important hours of her life. There were things she remembered—what she had told Faisal for one. But there were other memories that seemed to fade in and out. Things she knew were important and she hadn't told Faisal because they'd faded too quickly. She knew in her gut that knowing that time, reclaiming that last bit of her life might provide the one clue that would save her father's life.

She shuddered. She remembered everything that had happened at the hospital during the times she had been conscious. It was only the time before that, on the boat, that was in question.

She knew with a surety, that her father's reputation needed to be saved. She also knew that Faisal had been searching for her father. She had to help him and to do that she knew she had to go back to where it had all begun. She had to do it alone. She couldn't endanger anyone else.

She was certain of that, that and the face of a man she could now see in her memory. The threat to her father's life, the name of the town. All of it was engraved in her mind and all of it culminated in a strange little place, and a strange phrase. She'd heard him say it, Ben Whyte, her father's partner. She'd overheard him on the yacht when he thought he was alone. "A little piece of hell in the heart of Texas," she whispered. Whoever threatened her father, the secret to it all began there. Both her father and Ben had confirmed it.

She'd already shared with Faisal what little she remembered, including the names her father had given her. She couldn't share this new memory. She shook her head as if reaffirming her thoughts. He couldn't be involved. Already she and her father had been marked for death and it appeared only one of them had survived. She choked back a sob. Alive, dead, she was unable to hold a conviction either way on her father's plight. All she knew was that she needed to stop this before any more people died.

She'd had solid food since this morning but they'd

left the intravenous in to keep her hydrated as an extra precaution. The physician had spoken of having it removed today or tomorrow. Considering the time, she guessed it would be tomorrow. She couldn't wait. She looked at the intravenous tubing, at the needle in the back of her hand, took a breath and yanked. A sharp bite shot up her arm and then the needle dropped to the sheets along with a trickle of bright red blood. She took an end of the sheet, pressing it to the back of her hand and with the other hand she fumbled for a tissue. This was proving to be a messy endeavor. She didn't want to leave a trail of blood behind her. She pressed for a minute and then lifted the tissue. The wound was weeping more than bleeding. Good enough. Her legs shook. She took a deep breath and then another. She could hear voices in the hall. She lay back down and pulled the thin blanket to her chin.

The door opened.

She closed her eyes, sensed a presence and then heard the door click and opened her eyes. She was alone.

She waited, one minute and then two. She didn't have many minutes to waste. Her father needed her. And whoever wanted her dead would not stop. She wasn't sure how she knew that, but she knew that her being near anyone endangered them. She needed to get out, get to Texas and get her memory back. For it was only then that she could stop whatever evil had been set in motion that night on the yacht.

She pushed the door slowly open. The hallway

was quiet. She slipped out turning left past an empty staff room where she slipped in and saw the strap of a purse in a drawer. Someone had forgotten to lock up her purse or meant to come back quickly. She didn't think. She'd never done this before but she was desperate. Two minutes later she was out of the room with fifty dollars in her hand and was heading for the emergency exit. On the way down the utilitarian stairs she stopped at each floor. Three flights down there was a floor that appeared to be more for supplies than patients. It was there that she found a pair of scrubs and a pair of shoes. She changed right there in the empty, open hallway. It was her last stop before emerging on the bottom floor and into a back parking lot. She took a deep breath. Her heart pounded. She knew only one thing. She had to get out of here, out of Miami, out of Florida. Her memory was coming back and with it fear. She had to get far away, for there was one thing she knew for sure. The man on the yacht, Ben—wanted her dead. While her memory didn't give her all the facts, her gut told her that he would stop at nothing. She also knew that finding the evidence her father claimed existed was up to her— she was her father's last chance.

Chapter Eleven

Miami, Florida
Sunday, June 12—10:45 p.m.

Ava had ridden two city buses and fallen asleep on the second. Fortunately, she'd told the driver where she wanted to get off. Now, in a drugstore almost ten miles from Mercy Hospital and across the street from the intercity bus station, Ava looked in a small cosmetic mirror above the eyeshadow display. It was the first time she'd seen her reflection since this ordeal had begun. She grimaced at the tangled hair, the pallor of her face and the dark circles under her eyes. She was a mess. If nothing else, she needed to take a brush to her hair and add some life to her face with some cold water. But the only thing she could get here was a brush and maybe a tube of lip gloss. Then she remembered her financial state and dropped it all from her list. A finger combing was all she could afford for now. Later she'd wash her face in a public restroom.

She sighed and turned away from the mirror. De-

spite everything that had happened and maybe because of it, she was forever indebted to Faisal. It was
partially because of his generosity that she had enough
money for a bus ticket to Texas. But Faisal was always
very liberal with money, generous with his friends
and those he cared about. She remembered that from
her college days. Then, he'd paid for everyone's meal
on more than one occasion. And, when he'd thrown
a party, he'd paid for all the food and alcohol, even
though he didn't drink. He'd always been about what
everyone else wanted, what made them happy and so
he gladly shared his resources with others. To say he
had deep pockets was an understatement. His first gesture when they spoke had been to make sure that she'd
had enough money for snacks or books or whatever
she might need, including a meal in the hospital caf-
eteria if it came to that. It was one hundred and fifty
dollars. While he'd never know where her thoughts
had gone when she'd seen the money, she remembered the guilt of taking it. She also remembered the
desperation that didn't allow her to quibble over his
offer. Normally, she'd never have agreed but there was
nothing normal about this situation. She was in deep
trouble. She would never have turned to Faisal without
her father's suggestion, but she believed in her dad.
When, in the heat of panic and trauma, her father had
steered her toward Faisal, she'd never questioned it.
Then it had been different, a desperate situation. But
now, she could only think that Faisal was the boy she
had gone to school with. There was no way she would

involve him in the unidentified trouble she found herself in. It was bad enough that she might be in danger. She wouldn't have him in danger too. He'd rescued her and that alone was enough.

Despite what Faisal had given her, her funds were low. She could get to where she needed to go in Texas but she was going to be eating little once she was there. She'd needed more money. What she'd done to get it wasn't her. She grimaced at the thought of what she'd done, stealing money from someone's purse— she fully intended to pay the woman back with interest.

Theft. Her stomach clenched at the thought. But there was no going back. A change in shifts with the hallway temporarily clear had given her the opportunity to escape. She'd planned all of it. Evening was a slack time. Even her security took a break. With patients settled, medical staff tended to take their breaks, as well, and the hallways emptied.

From here on in she was in survival mode. She had to conserve what she had for the bus ticket out of here. She was ready to hit the road. She had a place in her memory but no purpose. She only knew that there were answers there and that she needed the memories to save her father or at the least salvage his reputation. A sob rose and stuck in the back of her throat. This was all so difficult. She wished she hadn't had to run from Faisal. He'd been so good and yet his presence had also brought back so many other memories. And her presence only put him in danger. She couldn't think of any of this right now. Instead, she focused on collecting her meager supplies. She bought water and energy bars. But as she went to the counter to pay, her vision blurred. She had to lean on the counter to get her equilibrium. But despite her efforts, the items still dropped from her hand onto the counter more forcibly than she might normally have intended.

"You alright, honey?" the clerk asked in a drawl that reminded her of where she needed to be and that time was slipping away. The clerk's hands were on her full hips and her face was heavily wrinkled and, despite what appeared to be too many years worshipping the sun, seemed to emanate motherly concern.

"Fine," she muttered. But she looked away as the world spun. She clung to the counter and took a deep breath. The world righted again.

"You're sure? I have daughters your age. I'd hate to think that if they were in trouble, someone wouldn't help them."

She couldn't take this much sympathy. She was either going to cry or pass out. She could do neither. This was all on her. There was no one to lean on, including this kind stranger. Instead, she took a deep breath and was finally able to meet the eyes that looked at her with so much concern that she almost wilted and burst into tears. She couldn't do that. She pushed back from the counter. She had to stand on her own two feet if she wanted to fix what was endangering her family. If she could only remember more.

"I'm fine," she repeated like a skipping vinyl record. "Really. Thank you."

The clerk looked at her for a second longer as if assuring herself of the truth of that and nodded as she
rang in her items.

Ava took a five from her pocket. The money felt
treacherous and wrong in her hand. A minute later,
she left the store with the few things she'd bought in
a plastic bag over her arm.

Her thoughts went to Faisal. He wanted to help.
She wanted to trust him but she didn't want to hurt
him. Somehow she knew that what she faced was better handled alone—without risking anyone else being
hurt, like her father.

Would he try to follow her? Knowing him, remembering what she knew of him—she knew he would.
At least he would try. That was why it was important
he didn't find out where she was going. She had no
connection to Texas, there was no reason to believe
she'd go there. It would be over before anyone could
find her. There was something else that nagged at her.
Her memory stalled. It needed to come back faster
and there was nothing she could do to change that.
She remembered her studies on amnesia. She'd never
thought to apply that small part of one semester to real
life, especially to herself.

She remembered that Faisal had mentioned something about her father on his last visit, but her memory
had still been incomplete. Now, her returning memories only made the danger that much more palpable.

Ben Whyte. The thought of him and what he'd done made fear run through her body so strongly that she wanted to throw up.

She needed to think yet somehow her most powerful resource was silent—all cylinders not a go. It was the worst time to be intellectually limping. She was running out of time to come up with a plan. Worst of all she needed to remember what it was that threatened her very life and what drove her to a little Texan town seemingly in the middle of nowhere.

She moved around the drugstore and to the parking lot. Two bins sat side by side. Could she be lucky enough that at least one of them was a used-clothing bin? There was no one near the bins and the lot on that side wasn't well lit. It was perfect cover. With a bit of luck no one would see her. She hurried over.

"It is," she murmured seeing the charity name on the bin. She raised the lid. The bin was full, another bonus. She could reach quite a bit of the clothing, at least what was on top. If it weren't this full, she would have been out of luck. Instead, she yanked out an oversize beige sweater. She dug as far as she could reach and pulled out a beige canvas bag. Beige seemed to be her color tonight. She dug some more and found a pair of jeans, much too large. She tossed them back and dug, finding a T-shirt. She looked down at her scrubs. They were brown. She had a matched set. There was no one around. In front of her were office buildings. It was after work hours and other than cleaners, they were quiet. She imagined that unless the odd cleaner looked out at just the wrong moment, it didn't matter if she changed here, no one would see her. Behind her was the drugstore, the side that faced her was windowless. She moved between the two bins and tore off the top that matched the scrub pants and replaced it with the T-shirt and then the sweater. She put her water and granola bars in the bag and put it over her shoulder. She tossed the shirt she'd been wearing into the bin. She didn't look great but she blended in with the general population a lot better.

She hurried back around the corner of the drugstore and across the street to the bus station. There, diesel fumes tainted the air and luggage littered the sidewalk. The fumes from the buses waiting beneath the lights that lit the area like daylight threatened to choke her. Half a dozen buses idled on the tarmac and only ten feet from her a wiry, gray-haired man was loading luggage into a bus's underbelly. Someone jostled her and she shifted away. The area was quickly becoming crowded with people as departure and arrival times intersected. Her heart pounded and she fought to look normal, like a young woman heading cross-country in a pair of scrub pants and a sweater. She looked down-and-out for sure but she was also boarding a bus in an area of Miami that couldn't be called well-off. A bus pulled in, next to one that was pulling out.

There was so much she didn't know. If she'd had access to a computer she would have checked her father's email. She knew it was a critical piece but instinct told her that her answers lay in a Texas town of negligible size and it was imperative she waste no time getting there.

She took a breath, fighting for normalcy. Yet nothing was normal. She was running on instinct. Still choking in a gray fog of memory loss, she was following her gut and it was screaming *run*.

She went inside to purchase her ticket.

Outside again, Ava coughed from the fumes and her eyes teared. She fumbled in the pocket of her scrubs for one of a handful of tissues she'd stuffed there before leaving the hospital. She knew, despite her change of clothes, that she looked a wreck. She'd tried hard to blend in but she'd been to hell and back, and she was still wobbly on her feet. To her right a black woman with gray hair stopped short, looking at her with what seemed like concern. Then she scowled. Ava turned away, her heart skipping a beat. She didn't need attention, sympathetic or otherwise. She moved a few feet away, putting distance and more people between her and the curiosity of the stranger.

She pushed deeper into the crowd. She was thankful the woman whose eye she had caught only minutes ago had disappeared into the queue for a bus marked Chicago.

A middle-aged woman in jeans and a blouse, who also had sunglasses perched on her head as if she were making a fashion statement, glowered at her. Ava drew herself up taller. She shifted tactics. The way to fit in was to believe you belonged here, that everything was right and that was the aura she'd exude.

She'd read that somewhere. This was something that she could never imagine happening to her. And yet it was. She was fleeing from a trouble she couldn't remember. She only knew that she needed to get out of this city. It wasn't safe and it wasn't the place where she would find the answers she needed, answers that would save her father.

In the meantime, she had to look like everything about her and her situation was normal. It was the appearance she had to portray even though she ran a risk of standing out even in her toned-down outfit.

Loud voices had her turning her attention to her right where a couple was arguing. She turned away. The crowd continued to jostle this way and that. It was her best defence, remaining out of sight hidden amid numerous people.

AN HOUR LATER, near the back of the bus and seated alone, at least for now, Ava took a deep breath. She went over the most recent events. It was a joy to savor the memories she did have. She couldn't believe her luck. But she'd whisked through purchasing a bus ticket and boarding the bus without a second look. Whether it was the late hour or whether identification wasn't needed, she didn't dwell on her good luck.

The memories were coming back and she wished for the first time that they weren't. They were hard and fast and intense, and they were worse than she could ever have imagined.

She was a witness to attempted murder. Her hands

shook at that thought, not so much at the knowledge, she'd always remembered that, it was the details that were slowly coming back. The sounds of the scuffle, the gun blast were clear in her mind. She'd already been in the raft but too far away. The waves had taken her twice the distance away. Finally, the vast ocean and the darkness had blanketed the distance between them and she'd been alone.

They'd been attacked that night on the yacht. Their attacker had never meant for her to get away. Her father's desperation in those last moments had made that obvious. Now, her father might be dead and that was something that she couldn't change. She needed to focus on what she could change, saving his reputation before the man who may have killed him stole that too.

FAISAL LOOKED AT his watch. It was just prior to midnight. The helicopter's spotlight showed nothing but the swell of waves. There was nothing to indicate that the yacht or any of its occupants had ever been here. He finger-combed his hair. His head ached from lack of sleep. He hated the thought of leaving Ava alone but he'd been assured that she would sleep through the night. That reassurance had galvanized him to go out on one more search. He'd hoped that, of all the searchers out here, he would be the one to find Dan Adams. It was ridiculous thinking. He'd had more than his share of luck when they'd found Ava. An hour later, he and the pilot agreed to call it a night.

Other volunteers took over where they had left off,

combing the ocean for what was really a tiny piece of flotsam in a vast ocean. It was five in the morning before he was back in his suite, which seemed empty and hollow. He lay down to grab a few hours' sleep before going up to the hospital to see Ava. She'd been scheduled for an X-ray first thing that morning, so there was no need to go in until that was complete. He managed three hours before his phone rang. He looked at the number and knew that everything was about to change.

Chapter Twelve

Monday, June 13—6:30 a.m.

Ben Whyte couldn't believe how easy it had been. He'd slipped in the crew entrance of a cruise ship heading from the Bahamas back to Florida. While at sea, a news report had confirmed that Ava Adams had been found floating in a life raft in the Gulf Stream somewhere off the coast of Miami. He didn't get the specific details because they didn't matter. He was almost giddy with relief. He controlled himself long enough to hear the rest, which only confirmed what he knew. She was thought to have been a passenger on the yacht owned by Dan Adams. The report also provided the information that Ava was at Mercy Hospital in Miami. It was all he needed.

He'd known it was a crazy idea to kill her here. He knew that he should wait for a better time. But desperation had driven him when he'd slipped by hospital security and gone up to Ava Adams's floor. Luck was on his side when the staff at the nurses' station were distracted by a doctor's arrival. He was able to slip by the station unnoticed. Within a minute he had made his way down the hallway.

When he'd entered Ava's private room, she was sleeping. Her face was turned away from him and her long dark hair covered what he might have otherwise seen of her face. He'd stood staring at her for a minute.

He took a deep calming breath and slipped the pillow out from beneath her head. She shifted in her sleep. Then he settled the pillow over her head, shifting the pillow to her face and pressing down as she woke up and began to scream. The sound was muffled by the pillow. Her struggles quickly waned and he easily held her down. Eight minutes later he was able to open the door and calmly walk away.

Dead, just like her father. He smiled.

As he walked down the hall, heading back to the elevators, he could hear the murmur of voices from the nurses' station. He paused and then kept walking. He had nothing to fear. He was a visitor like any other. But his heart pounded despite his mind's reassurances and he slowed his pace while he was within earshot but out of sight of the nurses' station. He was curious as to what they were saying.

"Stole fifty dollars from me." There was an edge to the speaker's oddly soothing husky voice. It was a sexy, morning-after voice and reminded him how long he'd been without. "I can't believe it. I wouldn't have thought it was her but she left a note." The woman laughed. "Promised to pay me back. Signed it Ava Adams."

"And took off just like that?" the other laughed. "I kind of like it. An escapee."

More muted giggles.

"They didn't waste any time filling her room."

"No. We're maxed out on patients this week. Had one in the hallway. An unacceptable situation."

Damn it, he thought. Was it possible? Had he killed the wrong woman? A shiver streaked through him. He'd killed only twice in his life before this. But both times had been justified. Now he wasn't so sure. Had he officially become a cold-blooded murderer, killing someone for no reason? A shudder ran through him. He'd become just like his brutal father, who had let his emotions, especially anger, rule his actions. He'd disappeared from his life, sentenced to jail, after killing a man in a barroom brawl. Ben had been six and glad to see him go. His father was the reason that he'd changed his name from Tominski to Whyte as soon as he reached the age of majority.

He wouldn't think of that—instead he had to focus on the now. He had to force himself to breathe, to calm down and to take a closer look at his surroundings, to act normal.

"I wonder if they'll find her?" the other nurse mused.

"I doubt if they'll look but I'd sure like my fifty dollars back."

"I can't believe that Ava Adams just slipped out of here—past us."

He walked faster, keeping his eyes ahead and only stopping at the elevator. He stood there like any other visitor, waiting for the elevator to arrive at his floor. Except he hadn't pushed the button.

"The authorities weren't called," the woman with the husky voice said.

"Fifty bucks is fifty bucks."

Neither of the nurses were looking his way.

He turned and headed to the stairwell without another thought to the woman he'd just killed. Ava was still alive and he needed to find her. He pushed open the door to the stairwell and felt the rush of cool air like a calming balm. Behind him, at the far end of the hallway where he'd so recently come from, he could hear hurrying footsteps and agitated voices.

He knew what that was about or at least he could guess. They'd found a patient dead. But they wouldn't know it was murder, not yet. He'd be long gone by the time that information was known. He'd propped her back on her pillow, leaving her lying there, still and not breathing. Nothing would show, at least not immediately, that he had leaned on that pillow with a good portion of his weight nor that she'd had no chance. She was doomed from the beginning. And she wasn't Ava.

Ava Adams needed to die and she needed to do it soon. He took the stairs at a run as if flying down the fire exit, possibly breaking his neck, would somehow take Ava out sooner.

Monday, June 13—8:00 a.m.

WITH HIS THOUGHTS on Ava, Faisal answered his phone with a more abrupt hello than normal.

It was Colin Vanstone. He was the hospital administrator. Faisal had had a few conversations with the man since Ava had been admitted. This time, Colin began the conversation without his usual niceties.

"I don't know how it happened. Ava Adams has left the hospital."

"What do you mean 'left'?" It seemed like time stopped, like he wasn't making sense of what the man was telling him.

"She's no longer here. But I can assure you that she was definitely not discharged. In fact, considering the shape she was in earlier, I'm surprised—"

"When? Where?" Faisal punched out the abbreviated questions as he cut the man off. He could feel the plastic of the phone creak under the pressure of his fingertips. He eased his grip.

"I'm sorry—"

"I don't need your apology," Faisal cut him off. "Give me the details and quickly."

He listened as the administrator relayed the few facts he knew. The facts turned out to be nothing more than a bed check that had turned up an empty room. There had been no sign of Ava anywhere on the floor. That was hours ago. Faisal couldn't believe it. Ava was missing. It was nothing that anyone had predicted or, in his defense, could have predicted. She wasn't in shape to run. She had shown no signs of that, only a worry about her father. He'd judged all of it wrong. This changed everything, in a way that was unthinkable. In fact, from what he could see, the case—what there was of it—was majorly compromised unless he could find her. And he'd better find her fast.

"I'm not sure how she escaped," Colin Vanstone admitted. There was a sheepish edge to his voice. "Although, even the security you had in place took breaks."

"Escaped." He frowned. As if she was being held prisoner instead of being kept safe. *Escaped.* Despite everything that had happened, the thing that was highlighted in his mind was the word *escaped.* It left an ugly taste in his mouth. Escaping was for convicts not for someone like Ava. She'd been a voluntary patient in an American hospital, not a dangerous criminal. All that aside, the thought of her alone on the streets of a big city like Miami in her state was inconceivable. She had no money, no transportation, no nothing and a faulty memory.

"It seems she disappeared several hours ago. The room has since been filled…"

"Filled?" There was a harsh edge to the word. He couldn't believe any of this.

"I wasn't notified until…" His voice trailed off as if he had more to say and yet was reluctant to add whatever it might be.

"What the hell?" he spat out, skipping over what

only appeared to be a lame excuse. "How did you let her get away?" He paused, realizing that what he had said had been contradictory to his thoughts about escape, but it didn't matter. What mattered was finding her. "When did it happen?" He had more questions that he wanted to ask. But there were only so many answers he was going to get, and none to the question of where she had gone. He was ready to move now. To get her back. He wasn't sure how this had happened. He'd never thought she'd run.

"Considering the circumstances, I discharged the security."

"Discharged the security..." His voice was slow and deadly as his mind tried to wrap itself around the massive screwup that had happened.

Faisal bit back his next comment. He didn't need to waste time on judgments.

"She was seen going down the corridor, alone. Last evening."

"Yesterday?" He couldn't filter the anger from his voice. This was unbelievable. He wanted to hurl the phone and go after her immediately. But that would be ridiculous. He needed the facts, he needed control.

"A volunteer saw her, they had no reason to question her, or, for that matter, report it. In fact, he wouldn't normally be there that late but he'd brought a magazine up to a patient. Then the ward clerk found the note..."

"What note?"

"She borrowed fifty dollars. At least that's what her note said. Opened an unlocked cabinet and took a fifty from one of the nurse's bags." The administrator cleared his throat. "I'm not sure how it happened. She wasn't under guard but—"

"She was your responsibility," Faisal snarled. He couldn't believe this, the why of it—nothing gibed. Where had she gone and why had she run? Had she felt threatened?

"What kind of shape was she in?" he asked. There were so many concerns here, not least of which was Ava's physical health. He remembered how she'd been when he'd last seen her. Weak, still confused and lying down.

"When she was last seen by a nurse at 9:30 p.m., she was awake and alert but her memory was still shaky. That's what the last charting reveals." He cleared his throat. "They'd given her solids but hadn't taken the intravenous line out."

"What are you saying?" He could only picture the needle providing sustenance directly into her vein—it had still been in. That meant…the thought dropped, it was an ugly visual.

The administrator cleared his throat as if his next words were difficult or at least reluctant. "She pulled it out and not well. There was a trail of blood on her bed sheets."

"She was bleeding?"

"Nothing major, the wound will naturally seal itself within a matter of minutes. Usually we apply pressure in the form of a cotton pad and a light bandage. I wouldn't worry about that."

"What do you propose I worry about?" Faisal asked. He'd left money for her in case there was something she needed at the gift shop, or for a meal at one of the hospital kiosks. He'd been generous in what he'd left—now he realized that he might have been too generous. He'd facilitated her escape. Like a fool, he thought as he fought the urge to hurl the phone. Instead he clenched his fist and directed his ire at the man who'd just given him the news.

"Seriously, this has never happened. When we've had patients in a hurry to get out of hospital care we've been able to convince them that it wouldn't be in their best interest," the administrator said as he skated over the damning words.

"Why not this time?"

"She gave no hint of her intention."

Smart, that was Ava. She'd kept silent and used that as a cloak to slip out under the wire. She'd obviously remembered something that she hadn't revealed to him.

Darn her, stubborn as he remembered, except now the playing field made the deception on her part all the more dangerous.

"I can't believe it happened. I mean the hallways are empty at times but this time it wasn't just the hallway that was empty but the nurses' station too. She literally lucked out."

She outsmarted you, he thought. It wasn't surprising. He remembered how wicked smart she was. She had gone on for an advanced degree long after he'd kicked formal education aside for a chance to work in the field and take the helm of the Wyoming office of Nassar Security.

His mind returned to the present. She might have some resources but she wouldn't have much. And she had no clothes. He couldn't imagine that she'd get far considering what she had available for a wardrobe. "What was she wearing?" Faisal asked, thinking of the sleepwear that he'd rescued her in and the equally inappropriate hospital gown.

"I couldn't tell you."

He should have expected that answer. "She couldn't leave in a hospital gown," he said, trying to keep the edge out of his voice.

"True but in a hospital it's easy enough to get your hands on a pair of scrubs. It's the norm to see them anywhere in the city—people coming and going from work. I'm not saying that's what she did, however."

Unfortunately, it was a valid point, Faisal thought grimly. The various hospitals and medical facilities in the city employed a huge network of people. Many of them dressed in the classic scrubs, from physicians to nurses and even students. It wasn't an uncommon sight even outside hospital grounds.

"There's more," the administrator said.

"Get to the point," Faisal growled.

"That patient, the one placed in her room, has since passed on. A tragedy. A young woman admitted for possible gall bladder surgery died before we could help her."

The blood seemed to roar in his ears. He wasn't sure if he was hearing right. "Ava's room was filled and that patient has since died?" he repeated the facts as he understood them. He wasn't sure how this could happen.

"Yes, it appears that way. An autopsy has been ordered. She was only twenty-eight and this was completely unexpected."

"What did she die of?"

"We don't know," Colin replied. "Could be a number of things. An aneurysm for one. It's rare but not unheard of."

"Foul play?" It had to be asked. Faisal was frustrated and not done with this man. Had Ava been the target?

"It's possible but doubtful." There was a slight hesitation in the way he said the words, as if he didn't quite believe them.

"Was there anyone around, anyone suspicious-looking?" Faisal didn't keep the impatience out of his voice. The man's methodical tone was driving him crazy.

"One of the nursing assistants saw a man at the elevator shortly before the body was found. Nothing was thought of it. He could be a visitor."

"What did he look like?"

"Middle-aged. Gray-streaked dark hair. Caucasian. Average height. She only saw him from the back."

"Anything else?" he asked and his gut told him that everything about this was wrong. Not just the murder, which was beyond wrong, nor the fact that Ava had disappeared, but there was something else, something even more deadly.

"The next patient was moved in immediately after we discovered the first patient, Ava, missing. The room was cleaned an hour after the discovery but the name hadn't been reassigned. It was still marked Ava Adams," the man said gravely. "I don't like what that might imply. The body is just being removed now," the administrator said in a regretful tone of voice.

Faisal's entire body was tense. His senses were on high alert. This information changed everything. The woman in Ava's room was dead, murdered, he was sure of it. Within hours of her leaving…it was beyond hope that the intended target had not been Ava.

The question was still who had killed and why, and more important, where was Ava now? And why had she run?

Five minutes later, Faisal disconnected with less information than he'd like. But considering everything that had happened, he doubted if the woman who had died in Ava's room had expired from natural causes.

Faisal clenched his fist. He sat for a minute staring silently into space. He could have been anywhere. He didn't see the elegant decor of the suite. He couldn't believe that Ava had regained her strength and potentially her memory and then coasted out of the hospital with an ease that bordered on the ridiculous. He needed to find her, like yesterday, and before someone else did.

Chapter Thirteen

It was less than an hour since Faisal had received that fateful call that Ava was missing. Now he looked long and hard at the face of the young woman who lay dead on the cold steel of the examining table. Her hair was long, almost to the middle of her back. She was brunette and a few years older than Ava. After that, the similarities stopped.

He'd insisted on viewing the body in the hope that the similarities would somehow give him a much-needed clue. Now he didn't know why he'd bothered. It was depressing and frightening all at the same time. Looking at her frightened him for Ava and saddened him for the deceased woman's family.

"She may have been asphyxiated," the coroner said.

He listened as the coroner went into some detail on why he believed that could be a possibility.

"Her eyes are bloodshot. Classic sign of asphyxiation."

A chill ran through him like none he'd felt before. He'd stood in this position many times but never had he felt the haunting fear that the person before him could have been someone he knew and loved. He almost took a step back. That thought combined with the cold steel and sharp smell of disinfectant that depersonalized death was almost too much. This wasn't Ava but someone had loved her.

Regret and anger snaked through him as he thought of how this young woman had died unnecessarily, how it could just as easily have been Ava on that slab. The reality was as disturbing as it was unthinkable. Whether they could prove it or not, he was sure that this woman had died of unnatural causes. It wasn't right or fair. And he knew it happened much too often. He'd thought of adding a branch of investigations geared solely to violence against women. He'd seen too much of it in his work. But now wasn't the time for such considerations.

Five minutes later, Faisal was heading across the hospital parking lot to a charcoal 1967 Mustang he kept in Miami for his rare visits to the city. He slipped behind the wheel and leaned back against the plush leather, the keys in his lap, his arms crossed and a frown on his face.

A woman who supposedly should have been Ava was dead. The fact that the decedent had been in Ava's room and Ava was still the registered patient indicated that Ava was the target. Now there were questions that needed to be answered, and quickly.

Where had Ava gone? He tamped down the panic

he'd felt at losing her when he'd only just found her. He had to stick to facts.

She'd come here for a vacation with her father before starting her working career as a clinical psychologist with a public school in Wyoming. But none of that gave him the answers he needed. She'd flown out of Casper, Wyoming, where she'd leased an apartment. It was interesting that she'd stayed in the state where she'd studied, at least for her first four years, and where they'd met. It was far from her father's residence in the Caribbean. But as much as he knew she loved her father, tropical life had never been for her, she'd said so often. So Wyoming, the end of school and the beginning of a career, was where her life had been until just a week ago when she'd joined her father in St. Croix for a voyage to the Bahamas. Now, her father was missing and she'd fled. To him, it was clear that she knew something and that she didn't trust anyone to help her. That pained him but he couldn't dwell on it. How he felt had no relevance to helping Ava.

He reviewed the facts, running them through his mind in record speed until he hit on what he considered to be key questions. Did Ava's secret threaten her father's well-being or his business? Yet her father was missing, possibly already dead, and still she'd run. Was it a threat that had frightened her? Did she know something? What had caused her to leave the hospital?

Whatever Ava was after, he was sure it was major and he was also sure that it was linked to the death in her room. He'd left the morgue with more questions than answers and an unspoken confirmation that Ava was no longer safe. She'd run and he thanked everything he cherished for that. If she hadn't, she'd be the one in that morgue.

Still, the fact that she'd run left him with questions. Why hadn't Ava turned to him instead of running? For whatever reason, she hadn't trusted him.

He opened the car door and stepped out. Despite the feeling of urgency, he had no direction. He needed to think this through. The door shut and he pressed the key fob, locking the door without a backward glance.

His mind went back over the case, of what he knew and what he might have missed. A yacht with what they could only assume had two men on board had disappeared. The Coast Guard had no answers and the vast Atlantic was hiding its secrets well. What had happened? What had Ava seen? He stood with his hands on his hips for a second, looking right, left and behind him as if on the quiet street there might be an answer. But all he saw was a pretty girl in a sundress walking a white poodle. Her long blond hair had stripes of baby blue. He'd like to tell her to dodge that salon the next time she had her hair done. It was a lighthearted thought amid the gravity of what had happened.

Faisal stared across the street where high-rises hid the vastness of the Atlantic. Somewhere beyond Miami's crowded docks lay a deadly secret. A secret that may already have killed.

FAISAL STOOD ON the sidewalk outside of Mercy Hospital considering his options. Ava's father's final destination had been Fort Lauderdale. He looked at his watch—it had been over an hour since he'd been told of her disappearance and it had been longer than that since she'd made her escape. From what he knew she might have had all night and had definitely had most of the morning. He'd like to grab the hospital administrator and shake sense into him. Instead he clenched his fist and tried to put himself in Ava's position.

What was in Miami for her? He couldn't think of anything. Where would she have gone? Her identification was missing, along with her credit and debit cards. The only money she had was the one hundred and fifty dollars he'd given her and the fifty dollars she'd lifted. Two hundred dollars wouldn't get you far, not if you wanted to sleep and eat.

A city bus lumbered by and stopped. He waited with the others at the stop and once inside, spoke to the driver. Two minutes later he stood on the curb. He now knew that there was a bus that went from the hospital to the intercity bus depot. It stopped here every fifteen minutes and arrived at the depot with one transfer. Ava could have been out of the hospital area within fifteen minutes of exiting the building. If that were true, she could be long gone. The problem was that, even if he was right, he didn't know where she was headed or why. He didn't know if a bus was the answer but it was a place to start.

Five minutes later, he was again behind the wheel

of his Mustang. He put the car in gear and with a screech of tires headed toward the depot. But an hour later he was ready to ditch the conversation with the man at the security desk. He was sun-bronzed and wrinkled with age, sun or both. He looked like he'd been working far too long. Worse, he refused to reveal any information. Instead, he stated that it was an infringement of traveler confidentiality and his oath of employment. Faisal doubted if he'd taken any oath of employment but whether he had or not, it was clear the conversation was going nowhere. He turned away in frustration but the feeling of eyes on him had him turning around. She was a plump woman somewhere between forty and fifty-five. Her brown hair was bobbed in an efficient shoulder-length style and she had a suitcase by her side. She seemed to be giving him the literal once-over—like she was deciding if she should trust him or not. Her lips tightened and she let go of the handle of her suitcase. It was as if she'd made her decision.

"I may know what you need," she said. The words sounded ominous and hollow like something from an old murder mystery, much like the tattered Agatha Christie in her hand.

He almost turned away—she could be an eccentric looking for a little excitement in her day. Judging from her flowered dress and the way she seemed at home, as if hanging around a bus depot was what she did, there might be a good chance of that. Yet his instinct told him to listen, and experience had taught him that evidence could come from the most unlikely places.

"I saw her, you know. The woman you're looking for." She put the book down as he closed the distance between them. "Gorgeous woman, at least I think she could have been but she looked sickly, frightened even. I didn't speak to her. She left here late last night." She looked at her watch and then sheepishly back at him. "I suppose I've lost track of time."

There was something about the fact that she never quite looked at him, and the way the ticket attendant had looked at her with disdain that made him doubt that the woman was a credible witness.

"Me, I'm headed here and there," she said vaguely, as if he had asked. "She got on a bus to Fort Lauderdale." She frowned and leaned forward. "You don't believe me?"

"I never said that." He'd put no thought into her last words other than Fort Lauderdale was where he had planned to meet Dan Adams. It was possible that Ava went there to find answers. He met the woman's bloodshot, brown eyes. The determined tilt to her chin seemed to say that she was going to make it despite her circumstances. "It's true. I don't know what her ticket read but that was the bus she got on. Hard woman to forget. If I were younger I might have been mighty jealous."

"Anything else?"

"Fort Lauderdale, like I said." She shrugged. "I'd love to go myself but funds are…" Her voice trailed off.

Faisal peeled off enough bills to get her across the country. "Here," he said simply. "Treat yourself to a trip."

Her eyes lit up as she took the money almost reverently. "My daughter lives in Chicago," she said simply. "I'll go there." And for the first time, there was purpose in her expression that made Faisal feel that she might not be the only one whose luck was about to change.

Reluctantly, he moved away. He looked at his watch—it was nearing noon. She could already have been there and left the bus depot heading for another destination. Enough time had passed. His phone buzzed.

"Zaf," Faisal said as he answered. "Things have changed direction here." He went on to tell Zafir how the occupant of Ava Adams's room had died, possibly murdered by suffocation. "One thing is clear—if it was murder, the murderer thought they were taking out Ava. The records hadn't been switched over, some foul-up at the front desk."

"So if it's murder, the murderer didn't know what Ava looked like," Zafir said thoughtfully.

"He knew alright. Thing is the victim had long dark hair and was close in age. If her head had been turned…"

"A case of mistaken identity."

"Unfortunate," Faisal said, "that anyone had to die. But what I have out of all of this is that the description the administrator gave of the man they think is the murderer matches Ben Whyte. He was the second man on the yacht that night."

"You're assuming he's alive. It could be a long shot but on the other hand, if he is you've got yourself a suspect."

"This case is not like anything I've seen before."

"I won't disagree with you there. My question is, what are the chances that Dan's still alive?"

"Not good," Faisal said grimly. "That's why, considering what's just happened, I'm focusing on Ava. Her safety is paramount. This death, it makes my skin crawl. Who would want to kill her?" He moved the phone to his other ear as he collected his thoughts and a breeze pushed a strand of dark hair across his eyes. He pushed it back impatiently.

"She knows something," Zafir said and there was a dark edge to his words.

"You're right about that. She had some traumatic memory loss when I saw her but eventually that's going to go away. Meanwhile, we've upgraded to a red," he said. He thought of the danger to Ava, which would also shadow him as he'd do anything to protect her. He'd do it for any client—but for her... He paused.

"Go out of touch—"

"And you'll send help," he interrupted. "Meantime, I'm heading to Fort Lauderdale."

"Dan Adams's intended destination."

"Exactly. But not just that—I had a tip at the bus station. Ava may be headed there."

He ended the conversation shortly after that. The

longer Ava stayed missing, the more Faisal worried for her safety. Especially now that he knew there was a killer on her trail, and she was running out of time.

Chapter Fourteen

Despite what Faisal had been told, there was no evidence that Ava Adams had gotten off at Fort Lauderdale. And there was no information to be found at the bus station in Fort Lauderdale. The man at security was no more helpful than the guy in Miami. In fact, he appeared to be more interested in the sandwich he was chewing than anything Faisal had to say. It took all Faisal had not to yank the sandwich from his hand. But instead he had to take the high road and walk—there might be information to be had, but it wasn't here or in this moment.

He stood outside for a moment and considered what he knew. Ava Adams had vanished. No one had seen a dark-haired, slim woman in scrubs. Faisal had asked every potential witness—the ticket agent, a number of other employees and a bus driver. No one had seen her. But it was possible that she'd disguised herself. Even a simple disguise, hair tucked up, a cap of some sort. The ditching of the scrubs—that is if she'd passed a clothing donation bin or similar such options. Providence could present all sorts of opportunities that one wouldn't notice in other circumstances. Desperation was a strong motivator.

His phone buzzed.

"What do you have, Barb?" He knew there was an edge to his voice but frustration did that. Whether Ava had been on a bus heading through Fort Lauderdale or whether she hadn't was still a question. As it stood, Ava had disappeared, leaving him concerned and beyond frustrated.

"Darrell Chan was the Vancouver man Dan Adams was in contact with a few times in recent days. He actually wasn't that hard to locate—I hacked into Adams's email and phone records and found him. Not too difficult to put two and two together. In fact, I think Ezra could have done it," she said, referring to her five-year-old daughter.

Despite the seriousness of the situation, there was a smile in her voice. Besides her efficiency, that was the other thing that made Barb so great to work with— her ability to add humor to any situation, even some of the toughest.

"I don't know, Barb, Ezra's smart but you're giving her a little too much credit," he said with a slight laugh that surprisingly, despite the situation, came naturally.

"Watch it or I may require babysitting duties again," she laughed. It was a standing joke between

them that in a pinch a few years ago she'd brought
Ezra to the office. He'd been in the office he used in
Marrakech that day and the little girl was fascinated
by the record player he kept on the filing cabinet. He'd
spent the last hour of the day sitting on the floor with
her tapping out the beat of "Smoke on the Water."
Barb had found the two of them there and never let
him forget it.

"Tell her we'll have another go next time I'm in
Marrakech," he said.

"I tell her that and she'll be begging you to show up
next week. She's smart but her patience needs some
work."

Faisal laughed. It made some of the more difficult
aspects of his job easier to have staff who knew him
well enough to know when he needed just a moment
of light diversion. A smile or a laugh to release the
pressure before he exploded from the stress he was
under, this time to save a woman he loved. And just
like that his lighthearted mood dissolved into the tur-
bulence of self-realization. His fist clenched the phone
so tightly he threatened to crack the plastic. Love. He
didn't love Ava, he couldn't. It wasn't true and yet his
heart told him that it was.

Barb continued, unaware of the revelation that had
just broadsided him.

"This thing just gets bigger the more I dig. I've
hacked one email that Chan sent. He seemed to be
under the impression that Dan was partnering with
Ben Whyte on land deals in a southern rural area of

Texas. Chan had already paid Whyte for one property and had reservations about the second. This all happened in a very short period of time. Thirty days. Interesting thing is that there's nothing filed online in the county land registry to verify any of this."

Faisal shook his head at what Barb was implying. But there was no denying the fact that Dan had mentioned land transactions when he'd called. At the time, the call had been brief and he hadn't gone into details. Still, he'd been surprised at the idea. Dan had never dealt in land before, not that he knew of. But real estate wasn't illegal and he hadn't given much more thought to it.

"Go on," he said as she paused as if waiting for confirmation from him.

"Here's what I have on Chan. He immigrated to Canada from Hong Kong while it was still part of Great Britain. Before it became an administrative region of China. As you know that all happened in 1997."

Faisal bit back a comment. He'd learned that it was quicker to let Barb say what she had unearthed without interrupting.

"For a decade or more prior to 1997, wealthy Hong Kong nationals were acquiring property in countries around the world as part of an exit strategy. The Canadian cities of Vancouver and Toronto were hotbeds for wealthy Hong Kong citizens to acquire real estate. Chan invested in real estate and owns numerous properties in Vancouver, mostly commercial."

"Anything else?"

"Not yet."

"Thanks, Barb," he said as he disconnected, smiling at the needless lecture on foreign affairs. But that was what made Barb so good. She never assumed you knew and she never wasted time asking the question if just flipping the information off would take less time. His mind switched to Chan. He wondered, since Chan lived a short flight away from Texas, whether he'd made the journey to verify his purchase or, more interesting still, whether he hadn't.

He wondered if there was a connection to what had happened on the missing yacht—a shady business transaction didn't seem likely. Dan Adams had always been a straight shooter.

He replayed in his mind everything Barb had said about Darrell Chan. The man had long since obtained a Canadian citizenship and established roots in the country. Considering the price of Vancouver real estate and the number of properties involved, Darrell Chan must be a very rich man.

An hour later, with all possibilities exhausted in Fort Lauderdale and no new clues as to Ava's whereabouts, he stood in the penthouse suite in the Nassar-owned hotel. Faisal contemplated everything he knew. He hated this part of the job, when he was forced to wait, to gather information before moving forward. When his phone buzzed, he grabbed it.

"I had to dig hard for this," Barb said. "Looks like Chan was fleeced."

"Fleeced?"

"He was sold a piece of land that was never going to be transferred as the seller didn't have ownership. Chan paid millions for a large tract of so-called ranch land. I found all that in a trail of emails in which he claimed Dan Adams was responsible as the seller."

"Unbelievable. I'm betting that's what the phone calls between Darrell Chan and Dan Adams were all about."

It looked like Dan Adams had been speculating in land, an area that he'd never shown an interest in before. In fact, he'd reacted with disdain the one time the subject had ever come up. Now he appeared to have done an about-face. More disturbing was the fact that there was evidence of fraud. Dan Adams had neither the heart nor the need to steal. Something much more sinister was going on. But despite knowing all that, he was stunned into silence. He could only listen to what Barb had found.

Sales of land in southern Texas. Purchases where no land had ever changed hands, nor would it. Ranch land sold to foreigners—*the perfect patsies*, he thought. They would arrive to discover there was no land and by the time they did the perpetrator would be gone. Dan Adams's name was on every deed. None of it made sense.

"Interesting thing," Barb said, "I've found no official record."

He hung up with a sense of foreboding. Something wasn't ringing true about any of this.

Monday, June 13—9:00 p.m.

THE GRIND OF the road, the sleepless night, all of it had exhausted Ava. She'd been on this bus for hours and there were hours left to go. The rest breaks had only made her wary and they proved more tiring than being on the actual bus. There, she was constantly vigilant, afraid that someone had followed her. Now, she slouched back in the seat trying to get comfortable. It didn't help. Despite cat napping through the journey, her head ached and her back hurt. The slight curve of scoliosis in her lower back ached as it always did without regular exercise. The nagging pain was the least of her problems.

On her head was a worn Chicago Cubs ball cap under which she had tucked her long hair so very little showed. She'd found the cap on the ground by the Miami charity clothing bin she'd raided before getting on the bus. She didn't think about who might have been wearing the cap before—couldn't. She was in survival mode.

A middle-aged man looked back at her from his place a seat ahead and across the aisle. There was a question in his eyes as if something about her bothered him. She knew her appearance was off, that she might appear lost or homeless in her worn, ill-fitting clothes. She hoped at worst she only looked down on her luck. She broke eye contact. Her psychology studies had taught her that the connection between strangers was fleeting. Memory happened when it was highlighted by an unexpected event or accentuated over a period of time or through repetition. She'd leave him nothing to remember. His ego and the memories that supported them were more relevant to his sense of self than she was.

She tapped her foot. The sneakers she was wearing pinched her feet, but there'd been no choice. They were the closest to her size in the hospital locker room. She felt bad. Someone would be going home in her work shoes.

She ran the back of her hand across her eyes, sweeping away dust, sweat and the remnants of the tears that the thought of her father always brought on. The air-conditioning seemed to barely move the air and the heat was cloying. She lurched in her seat as the road got rough for a minute and then settled into its regular rhythm. They'd encountered a detour only an hour ago and the ride had become slow and bumpy as they took a narrow, paved side road.

She looked out the window but there was nothing to see but the occasional sweep of blacktop, a road sign lit up by the headlights and darkness. She thought of Faisal. He'd been at the hospital every day, sometimes for hours. Once, she wasn't sure, but she thought he might have stayed the night. She remembered waking up in the night and seeing him there watching her. He had made her feel safe, feel like it would all work out, that her father—she turned her head to the window. She couldn't think of her father. It was all too grim, too seemingly hopeless. There was only his memory that she had to preserve, to make right. To ensure that his reputation and the charities he supported would remember him as the outstanding and upstanding man he was.

She tore her mind from the grim thoughts and instead her thoughts returned to Faisal. Seeing him again only reminded her of how much she'd missed him and of how much she still cared. It had been difficult not to tell him of her new memories, not to trust him. But that was the problem, she did trust him and she didn't want to place him in danger. Despite the years they'd been apart, she cared about Faisal too much. It seemed like both yesterday and so long ago since she'd seen him. Over the last few years, he'd never been far from her mind but her studies had been more important. At least that was what she had told herself as the years had slipped by. But he'd never left her heart. The hard truth was that she'd lost track of Faisal but she'd never forgotten him. She'd picked up the phone so many times to call him but she'd never known what to say. It had all been so long ago. A time when she'd felt things for him that she shouldn't have felt for a friend. They were feelings that she'd had to hide, for then Faisal had a girlfriend. She imagined it was the same now. He'd matured into an extremely handsome man.

Emotions aside, the smart thing would have been to trust him. He'd rescued her and she knew he was an investigator. Protecting people was his job. Knowing that didn't change how she felt. She couldn't involve him. She didn't know what she was up against and neither did he. Her father was more than likely dead. The thought of that again brought tears to her eyes. She couldn't jeopardize anyone else no matter who they were or what they did for a living. The only way to stop this was to uncover whatever it was that her father claimed was hidden in the small town where she was headed. She needed to go into her father's email, which he had shared the password for, just in case. But there'd been little time and no computer easily accessible, at least so she'd thought at the time. Her mind hadn't been clear then. The email was important, she knew that. It was the first thing she'd check when she arrived.

"Just in case something happens to me," her father had said after giving her the password to his email.

Something had happened. She wiped away a tear. The only good that had happened in the last hours had been the return of her memory.

"Miss," an older woman said in a muted, nighttime voice as she stretched her arm across the aisle and held out a small packet of tissue. "You look troubled."

"I'm fine," Ava said, glancing briefly at the woman who had gotten on the bus at the last stop over an hour ago. The last thing she needed was attention of any kind.

The woman shook her head as if she were reading between the lines and seeing everything that Ava was trying to hide. "It will get better. No hardship lasts forever. You'll see."

"Thank you," she managed but the woman's compassion had almost caused her to break. She couldn't allow that to happen. She had to get it together. It was all on her and in getting to a small town in the middle of nowhere. To save her father's reputation she needed to be there. But to be any help at all, she needed to get it together as quickly as possible.

Two hours later, she was thanking the Fates that brought strangers into your life. For the woman turned out to be a lifesaver. Her name was Anne Johnson and somehow she made the fear, without ever knowing that it existed, manageable. She talked about her family, of mundane things—her sister who was waiting for her. Her voice was the kind that was soothing, a Southern drawl that was filled with life experience. She spoke briefly of her four grown children.

"All of them older than you," she said. "Six grandchildren so far."

The conversation went on—one-sided as it had been from the beginning. Eventually it faded as the night thinned, and as dawn broke they reached the stop that was Anne's. She felt a sinking feeling in her gut as Anne got up, grabbed her overstuffed flowered carryall and reached over to squeeze Ava's shoulder. Her smile was wide in her dark, round, rather plain face.

"You'll be okay," she assured. "And if you're not, you know where to find me."

Where to find me.

The thought that she might have to do that. That

she might need Anne's help. That fear found her and rode with her the last miles until a small town in Texas glimmered in the distance, offering hope with a good dose of fear.

Chapter Fifteen

Faisal put a call in to Aaron Detrick, an undercover operative with the Royal Canadian Mounted Police, or RCMP. He'd gotten to know Aaron when he'd had a case over three years ago that had involved a suspect crossing into Canada. Aaron and he had worked each side of the border to keep his client safe. That work had provided him some insight into the Canadian system and a fantastic contact in law enforcement.

He left a message for Aaron to give him a call.

Ten minutes later the phone rang.

"Aaron," he said. At any other time he would have been pleased to connect with him again. It was only distance and busy lives that had kept them from becoming better friends.

"You had a request in about Darrell Chan?" Aaron asked after they'd put in an abbreviated version of pleasantries. "I assume this is a secure line," he said without question.

"You know it," Faisal replied. "I was wondering if there's any record on him. Anything at all."

"Surprised that you ask. We've been trying to tag him for a long time. The guy is strange. Not in a personality type of way but in the way he dances between good and bad. He's made millions in Canadian real estate, is one of those types who's seen as a good guy, but is actually someone who will kill if you get in his way. The force," he said, referring to the RCMP, where he served as a detective sergeant, "has been trying to nail him for half a decade now. But he's slippery. He runs a mega real estate enterprise. He immigrated with money and has made another fortune in Vancouver. I expect you know the details of that."

"No. Actually, I'm just starting to get an idea of what he's about," Faisal replied.

"In the past he's run into a few glitches in business, shall we say. Deals that aren't quite what they seem. In two cases that we know of for sure, the people suspected of the crime against him have died. Not at his hands and not by anyone we can pin. There's a widely held belief within the force that it's the work of hired killers."

"Hired by Chan?"

"That's what I'd like to say we know but there's no evidence linking the killings to him. The way things came down, when you apply logic—well, in my opinion, it points straight at him. Without evidence, he continues to get away with murder. And he does it by hiring hit men, basically scum, but murderers nonetheless."

"Dangerous only when crossed."

"Exactly," Aaron said. "So what's going on there?"

Faisal explained what he knew. He told him about the calls that Chan had made to Dan Adams. "There's no evidence to say there's any wrongdoing," he was quick to add.

"Except for the fact that Dan Adams is missing. Of course, that's not saying anything," Aaron said. "I ran a CPIC on Chan, like you asked, and it came up clean," he said. He referred to the Canadian Police Information Centre's database. The database held criminal record information on Canadian citizens. This wasn't the first time that Faisal had asked for such a favor.

A few minutes later, he hung up.

Later with the lights of Fort Lauderdale spread out like a rich blanket beneath him, in another penthouse suite much like the one he left in Miami, Faisal checked the weather report. That's when things went from bad to worse. For now it appeared that the coast of Florida might get the brunt of Hurricane Dexter.

Tuesday, June 14—6:30 a.m.

AVA TOOK A deep breath as the bus passed the sign for Tristan, Texas, population 2,001. It would be a relief to get off the bus. But arriving at her destination was overwhelming. Her stomach heaved as she faced what felt like the moment of truth. She tried a trick she'd learned a long time ago, diverting her thoughts to something inane. She wondered who the "one" in the population sign was. Was it the most recent birth in town, maybe the only one this year? But the light-hearted thought didn't change her mood or the dark reason she was here. Once the bus came to a stop, she stood up, feeling underdressed and underprepared. She was darn close to helpless. This was the last place she knew her father planned to visit before he left for that fateful yacht trip that... She wiped the corner of her eye with her forefinger. She couldn't think of the fact that her father had more than likely died at sea and his reputation was about to be destroyed if she wasn't successful. It all seemed so surreal, everything that had happened these last few days. She felt like she had been moving in a cloud.

She remembered what her father had said on the yacht about Ben. He'd told her how he had backed Ben financially in a bid to help him get a footing in a real estate business. Ben was a man he'd met through his church, a man who was down on his luck or so he'd thought until he'd discovered that Ben was lying to him.

She grabbed her bag and dispensed with her thoughts. She needed to focus as she took her first look at her new temporary residence. The bus depot at Tristan was nothing like the one in Miami or any of those that had followed. It was small and worn, the paint peeling from the wall of the waiting area. As Ava stepped off the bus, the first thing that hit her was the heat. The temperature had soared since yesterday. Barren land with scrub brush stretched out to the north and south. In front of her were the worn edges of Tristan. The sign for a Flying J truck stop was visible about a half block away, along with a couple of motel signs. When she looked behind her, she could see a stretch of dry, desert-like prairie. She knew that the answer to what had happened on that yacht lay in this little community in a faraway corner of Texas.

She needed money. What Faisal had given her, what she'd taken—guilt made her pause—was almost gone. She needed more. This time she'd acquire it through a job. That meant short-term, menial labor.

She swung the mostly empty canvas bag over her shoulder and stepped out of the station. She blinked as the sun beat down on the blacktop. Her view of the town from here wasn't much. Trailers crowded together on one side. Commercial buildings with wire-fenced yards, cars in one, tires in the other. A number of motels just ahead, all low-rise, peeling paint, low-end. It was exactly what she needed. She headed toward the last in the row.

"This isn't going to be the Marriott," she murmured to herself as she remembered vacations her father had taken her on. He'd always been generous that way, taking her on no-expense-spared holidays throughout her life. She shook her head. She lengthened her stride. The sooner she got settled, the sooner she could help her father. Hopefully save him, she thought, clinging to the hope that he lived. But the odds of that were slim. Now there might well be only her and Ben, the man who wanted her dead. If she wanted to live, she had to find the evidence that he'd kill to hide.

Chapter Sixteen

Tristan, Texas
Tuesday, June 14—9:30 a.m.

As Ava stepped into the quiet confines of Tristan's only library, she was hit by the haunting edge of nostalgia. The smell of books reminded her of academia and her career that had yet to begin. It reminded her of her past studies, of everything that in the last few days had seemed lost. In fact, in the face of her new reality, they *were* lost. There was only the nightmare that she somehow had to wade through without getting anyone else hurt. Despite that thought there was something…someone, actually, who emerged out of the ashes of pain—Faisal. Ironically, now when she needed him most, she'd turned her back on him. But she'd had no choice. She'd cared about him too much. She'd thought about him too often through the last years when school had occupied her life in a way she knew few other periods of her life could. It was strange how psychology had turned her into an old soul with a knowledge that someone her age should not have. Again, she was diverting herself and her thoughts, and ultimately her need for Faisal. She'd never forgotten him and now she'd run, leaving him behind in the hopes of keeping him safe.

She pulled her thoughts from the past and from Faisal with difficulty. She had to face the present and the unknown if she were to stop whatever evil had taken out her father and could very well hurt others she loved. She had two names. She knew Ben Whyte had tried to kill her father. She also knew that the evidence for the land deal that implicated her father was filed here in Tristan—at least that's what her father had told her. The second name was Darrell Chan; she knew nothing about the man, except that her father had said in the event of tragedy to tell the authorities about him. She had—she'd told Faisal. She regretted that. It endangered him by giving him another degree of involvement.

She pushed the thought from her mind. On a back table a stack of books sat beside a thin, gray-haired woman who glanced up once from the computer terminal and then returned her attention to the computer.

"Can I help you?" The librarian smiled and Ava tried not to stare at the woman's thin lips, which were generously coated with red lipstick and stood out like a slap in the face. Her hair, bobbed at the ears, was a no-nonsense cut. That look clashed with the lipstick's attempt at glamour but her blue eyes smiled with a vibrant youthfulness.

If her problems had been simpler, the look and the attitude would have made Ava feel at home. As it was, she was on edge, well aware that she had little time. There was so much to do and it was already midmorning. She still had to find a job. The twenty-five dollars she had left weren't going to carry her far and she needed to eat. Her stomach growled as she thought of food. She'd had little of that. A loaf of bread and a jar of peanut butter had been her only purchase this morning and the groceries were tucked in the canvas bag over her arm.

Ava Adams had disappeared in favor of Anne Brown. It was a plain name that suited her current situation and had been inspired by the woman who had been so kind to her on the bus.

"I'd like to buy some computer time."

"No charge," the librarian said. "The town is trying to get more people online. The locals are notoriously cheap and sometimes I think that half of them might really believe in the rise of the machine. *The Terminator*, loved that movie," she said in response to what Ava knew was a slightly blank look. "Look, sorry, too much information." She gestured to two terminals, one that was occupied, the other free. "Help yourself. Call me if you need assistance."

"I will, thank you," Ava said. She went to the terminal, which was in a far corner of the library away from both the librarian and the woman who seemed to be the only other patron in the library.

She pretty much knew that she was fishing in the

dark. But she had nothing else but the knowledge that this place was the beginning of it all. What beginning that might be she didn't know. Hopefully, there was some clue to it all in her father's affairs. She opened his private email account. She'd told her father often enough to kick the email and move into more secure messaging methods but he'd been old-school that way.

He'd hinted that he was ready to take her advice two weeks ago. That was when he'd given his account password to her. It had been a casual mention, as though saying nothing would ever happen but he wanted to tell her anyway. He'd said that if something happened to him, she should access his email. At the time she'd thought that it was only because he was close to hitting a landmark birthday, shortly after hers, and he was feeling his own mortality. Now it meant so much more.

As she clicked through the various emails, she felt less like she was intruding into her father's private life than she'd thought she would. There were more business-related than private emails. They were emails concerning various meeting results, a response from a birthday greeting to a woman she knew had acted as his assistant.

Five minutes in she was frowning as a name kept reappearing. Darrell Chan had sent her father a number of emails in regard to ranch land he had purchased in the area.

The correspondence was antagonistic, about a complaint that didn't seem quite clear. They were messages that seemed mired in secrecy as if there was a code being used. None of it, including the land mentioned, made any sense. Her father was a man who had been involved in a variety of businesses in his day. But he'd always had a particular loathing for real estate ventures. It had something to do with his own childhood growing up with a father who was what he liked to call a slumlord. As a result, or so he claimed, he had no use for investing in real estate. Therefore, land transactions weren't something her father would be involved in—until now, apparently.

A shiver of foreboding ran down her spine. She'd never felt so alone. And for a second and then two she let her mind wander to a place of safety and that took her immediately to Faisal. She wished she could talk to him. More than that, despite her actions, she wished he were here. She remembered the way he had looked at her the last time she'd seen him. She could have melted into his arms but she hadn't acted on that or even admitted it. In truth, she hadn't been in any condition to act on such feelings. She pushed the thoughts from her mind. What she felt for Faisal had no place here.

She opened another email. There Darrell clearly stated that he wanted his money back. It seemed that he was beginning to believe that he'd been duped. She scrolled down. There was nothing else, no further correspondence. Nothing sent by her father, nothing received. And the date of the last email was the same as that fateful night on the yacht.

"What did you get involved in, Dad?" she whispered. Whatever it was, Ben Whyte and that ill-fated night on the yacht were now looking like they might be the climax of a deal gone terribly wrong.

A few minutes later she closed the account and after asking the librarian where land deeds were registered, she was directed to a small office down the street. A half hour later she left that office realizing that this was much worse than she imagined.

"Fai, what would you do?" she murmured as if he were by her side. Her father's name was signed on the transfer of the very land that Chan had insisted he'd been sold. Worse, the signature in her father's name was not his, it was forged. She was sure of that. She'd seen her father's signature often enough. Now, she clutched the copies of two land transactions that the clerk had given her. She was exhausted and she still had to fulfill her last promise to her father—to stay alive.

Chapter Seventeen

Fort Lauderdale, Florida
Tuesday, June 14—11:00 a.m.

Faisal's phone buzzed.

"I've been digging into land deals in rural Texas," Barb said. "Like you asked."

"Did we confirm my suspicions?"

"Not exactly. What I did find was that Dan had a number of calls in recent weeks from Ben Whyte. He was calling from a small Texan town—Tristan. So I checked into the place. It's a going-nowhere-fast kind of place. Stopover for truckers and such heading for bigger centers. Nothing much goes on."

"Strange," Faisal replied but his heart sped up slightly as it always did upon receiving a major clue. His gut told him that was where Ava had gone. His logical mind told him that he had no other options, no clue, no direction. He had to follow the clue he had or remain in a state of inertia. The latter was no more comprehensible than it was feasible. The problem was that he was pretty sure Ava wouldn't be using her own name but he had no idea what she was calling herself now. He had to go back to the bus depot and see if somehow repetition would provide the break he needed. The only thing he could do was ask employees, fellow passengers even, whoever might have seen her. But none of the passengers would know her name, so that only left employees. And so far, he'd struck out in dead-end Fort Lauderdale. It was beyond frustrating. He needed someone who remembered her boarding the bus. So far he hadn't received that break.

"Also, one other thing. I've had an eye on Darrell Chan," Barb said, breaking into his thoughts. "He's landing in Hong Kong International Airport as we speak. Seems our boy is flying the coop while he can."

"Interesting."

"That's not all," Barb said with barely a pause. "I've got evidence that he bought more than one tract of land near Tristan, Texas. A huge spread. There's no evidence of a monetary transaction other than a small initial deposit."

"Who did he purchase it from?"

"There was nothing about the sale online. The only evidence I have is an email from Darrell to Dan."

"I wonder if the land even exists."

"I wondered the same," Barb replied. "False deeds, pretty easy stuff. Hard part, from what I can see, is not getting caught. Darrell Chan was promised acres of land. Oil rich, at least that was what it was advertised as and all of it in south Texas. That's what I'm getting from hacking into more of Dan Adams's emails, but, like I said, none of this is registered in online records."

"Damn," he said shocked at what she said. "I can't believe it." In fact, he didn't believe it, at least not that Dan was voluntarily involved. He believed a lot of things but something like that of Dan, no.

But opinion wasn't proof and he'd need proof to nail Dan Adams's killer to the wall.

Any proof he needed was in Tristan, Texas. He clenched his fists at the thought that if Ava was there she was alone and without his protection. He needed to get there as soon as possible.

This time when he contacted security at the Miami bus depot, he got action. Security agreed to check the video. Thirty minutes later he knew that a woman matching Ava's description had been there. Her ticket would take her to the small southern town of Tristan, Texas. The estimated time of arrival was five hours ago.

He hung up shortly after that. He dashed the back of his hand across his forehead before grabbing his go-bag. He'd never felt anything so urgent in his life as the need to reach Ava. The story was piecing together quickly and he liked none of it. What he believed was that the truth had come out that night on the yacht and Ava had been witness to it all. He needed to get to Tristan, Texas, without delay.

Two minutes later he had the chopper on alert. Fifteen minutes after that he was preparing to board.

BEN WHYTE STUCK out his thumb and an hour later realized that getting another ride would be a long shot. The semi driver had just dropped him off. The hours on the road hadn't been kind. He no longer looked safe, nonthreatening. He was scruffy-looking, a middle-aged man with an after-five shadow and a wild look in his eye. No one else was going to pick him up. He ran his fingers through his hair, took his mind from what he couldn't fix, such as the beginnings of a beard, and plastered a goofy smile on his face. His lips ached from the effort and he couldn't bring a smile to his eyes but a few cars slowed, hesitated and then changed their mind and sped up. A few minutes later, he had success. A battered blue Cougar, a dream car for a car enthusiast, slowed down and pulled over. He eyed the Cougar, thinking of the possibilities. It was a car that one would fix up, that… His thoughts broke off as he concentrated on the smile, focusing on making the smile reach his eyes. The man who'd stopped for him might be a decade younger. He had artfully disheveled hair and a carefree look in his dark eyes.

He smiled, all the while thinking that soon he could quit with the idiotic smile that was killing his facial muscles. His lips actually hurt from the effort but it had paid off.

"You need a lift?"

"I do," he said calmly as he opened the door and slipped in knowing that this time he needed to take control. He was too close to his goal. No more sitting in the passenger seat and watching the miles go by. He didn't need a witness this close to his goal.

Ten minutes later he was at the wheel. It had been surprisingly easy. There was truth in everything getting easier with practice. This time he hadn't felt anything. It had been rather unreal. There'd been little blood in the kill. A sharp whack with the wrench he'd stuffed into his bag earlier. He followed the assault with a second blow just to ensure that he'd done enough frontal lobe damage to kill the driver. A bathroom break on the shoulder of the road, five minutes into the ride, had given him the opportunity. He supposed the element of surprise had given him the advantage but Eric hadn't been much of a fighter. By the time he'd realized—seen the wrench Ben held in his left hand that he'd conveniently picked up at the gas station—it was too late. There'd been a panicked look in his eyes when he'd realized what was coming down. Now, the seat was wiped clear of any blood with a jacket he'd found in the backseat. He'd thrown that into the ditch along with the body of his Good Samaritan.

There's no such thing as do-gooders, boy. It always turns out wrong. That had been one of the last pieces of advice offered by his father. It was the best thing that no-good piece of crap had done for him.

"No such thing," he repeated as he cranked up the radio and tapped a hand against the wheel as AC/DC's "Highway to Hell" beat at top volume. He floored the vehicle. He needed this deal done before the buyer became suspicious and Ava spilled what she knew. If she knew what he suspected she did then there was only one place to be, Tristan. That's the only place where the records were accessible for they weren't online. But no one was going to access them, he'd make sure of that. Then, once it was done and Ava Adams was dead, he was getting the hell out of town. He would be out of the country before Darrell Chan put a hit out on him.

Now he had to get to the place he'd once called home, back to where it had all started and where it would all end. He couldn't get there fast enough. Everything he was, everything he'd be—it all rested in Tristan, a little piece of hell in the heart of Texas.

Chapter Eighteen

Thank goodness for small towns, Ava thought as she briskly pulled the sheets off a bed. She loaded them onto her cart that was sitting just outside the door. The roar of diesel was a reminder that this town might be small but it was also a stopover for truckers. Fleets of them passed on the side roads as they took a break before heading to the bigger centers. She mused about how in a city she would never have been hired without any credentials. That was a good thing as she couldn't haul out her list of academic accreditations. None of her diplomas would do her any good here. Fortunately, in this small town in the south of Texas no one had given a thought to asking her for identification. They needed the help and she needed the employment. She'd never worked in the service industry. She'd been lucky. Her father had insisted she keep her mind on academics, and with the exception of her tutoring, a salaried job, no matter how part-time, was not a consideration.

Not wanting to arouse suspicion, the story she had told the motel owner of her reason for a lack of belongings was one of tragedy. Her home had flooded following a torrential rain. The disaster that followed caused her to leave her rental unit behind. She'd managed to leave the place unnamed and vague, rather like her memory had once been. The woman who managed the motel had asked no questions, only expressed sympathy. She'd felt beyond guilty about that but she had no choice. She'd make up for every shady thing she'd done when it was all over. That is, if she lived to see the end of this.

She'd been hired at noon and outfitted by one o'clock. It had been a stroke of luck when the woman who would have worked this shift had gone home sick. She'd even been given an advance on her paycheck. She'd had to ask and churn out an addendum to her hard-luck story and, frighteningly enough, that hadn't been too difficult. With a little tweaking, her real story was every bit the hard-luck case, so she wove bits of it into the story she'd already told. In fact, the story was so good, she'd surprised herself at her desire to keep embellishing. It wasn't a habit she was going to keep once this was over. In fact, she was surprised that the story had worked, that the woman who ran the motel had agreed to a small advance in exchange for her beginning work immediately. It wasn't much, but it was something.

BEN WHYTE'S HEAD hurt like hell and anger coursed through him. He eased his grip on the steering wheel when his knuckles started to ache. He'd get that little witch who could ruin his plans.

He needed Darrell Chan to pay up for the land he'd signed on to buy. It was the biggest deal ever and the one he needed in order to be able to call it quits. Once he had the money he would leave the country and everything else behind. He didn't need Dan Adams's interfering daughter ruining it all with something as simple as the truth.

It was here, in this out-of-the-way place, that all his dreams would come true. That's what he'd thought only weeks ago and then Adams had done what he hadn't anticipated. He'd thought their partnership was solid and he'd been proven wrong. Adams was never supposed to find out the truth and yet somehow he had. He'd had no choice but to take him out. With Adams out of the way, he hadn't expected another piece of flotsam—his daughter. By the time he'd realized that Ava Adams was on board, it was too late. Adams managed to get her off the yacht and out of his hands. She was a fly in the ointment and he wasn't sure what she did or didn't know. But if Dan had told her anything, he would have told her where the evidence could be found and that was here in Tristan. He had to make sure she wasn't here and if she was, he had to find her. If she was here, he was betting that she hadn't gotten farther than the outskirts of town.

He pulled down a service road, passed a filling station and then a junkyard piled high with rusted cars and assorted farm implements. Like many small towns where businesses had been shut down, a cluster of metal and pipe from projects long forgotten sat abandoned along with gas stations on either end of town serving travelers that never made it to the town center. A police cruiser drove slowly by, the officer glancing at him curiously. He nodded but didn't smile. He'd found eye contact and a friendly, but not too friendly, demeanor worked best with the local authorities.

He turned left into the rutted and worn blacktop of the motel's parking lot. He'd been to three others like it. But this time as he walked out of the administration office, he knew that he'd hit gold. It wasn't the same name but there weren't a lot of twenty-something women checking into motels in this town, not that matched her description. She was here. He touched the gun hidden beneath his shirt. He'd gotten not just a car but a gun when Eric had picked him up. The boy had been sheer gold.

Ava Adams, the name was like nails on a chalkboard. She knew too much and she was too smart. She was lethal in her own way and she needed to be removed just like her father had been. Unfortunately, he didn't have any time to drag it out, to have any fun. It was a shame because he wanted her in every way a man wants a woman. He wanted just one shot at her before she died.

Chapter Nineteen

Tristan, Texas
Tuesday, June 14—6:00 p.m.

Close to Tristan, Texas, and still in the air, Faisal received a grim lead. The radio was playing and a news report came on. One of the top stories was about a man being killed after picking up a hitchhiker. Motorists were advised to be on the lookout for a middle-aged Caucasian male about five-ten...

The report went on. Faisal had heard enough. His gut told him that the hitchhiker was Ben Whyte. But the interesting thing was that he'd murdered and stolen someone's car while hitchhiking.

He couldn't believe what he was hearing. He phoned the Houston Police Department and asked to speak to Detective Morris. Rex Morris was another law enforcement officer he'd dealt with before. He was open-minded as long as you didn't try playing any games with him. Even though it had happened outside Rex's jurisdiction, ten minutes later he had the details he needed. The death had been particularly violent. A wrench, wiped suspiciously clean of even a fingerprint, had been found in the ditch. The coroner had been on the scene and was convinced that the bludgeoning marks were fairly indicative that the wrench had been the weapon. In the meantime, the authorities would lift whatever DNA they could. Unfortunately, there was nothing solid to go on. All they had was a description of the vehicle the victim had been driving and an APB was out. He gave a brief description to Rex of the case he was on. They hung up with an agreement to notify each other if the vehicle was found. There was nothing else. He had to take the tip he had and run with it.

His phone buzzed.

It was Barb with the information he'd asked her to follow up on. Ben Whyte's mother's location. She'd found Evangeline Tominski's address and phone number in Chicago. He knew that this wasn't going to be an easy call and he was proven right minutes later. The woman sounded worn and beaten like she'd been a victim. If he could have painted a picture of the trajectory of her life, he guessed that it would have been done in gray with splotches of red—dull with moments of great trauma. It was sad and disheartening. Listening to the story of someone beaten down all their life was one of the few things that made him regret his career choice.

She'd opened up as soon as he'd told her who he was and that he was looking for her son. He listened patiently as she told him that her son, Ben Whyte, had supported her with an occasional check that he mailed to her. She said many things, many of them irrelevant but some very relevant, including how she was terrified of her son. She muttered that he was violent and had beaten her up many times. She said that she was afraid that he'd turn worse, kill even, just like his father. She then mentioned that some of it was her fault. She hadn't left his father even when he'd pushed the boy down the stairs in a fit of rage. Her son had limped ever since. And still she'd stayed until her husband had turned that anger outside the family and been jailed for murder. It had been an entirely disturbing telephone conversation. Sometimes, there were aspects of this business he detested. This conversation was one of them.

Knowing what had shaped Ben Whyte gave him a clearer picture of who he was dealing with. He bet that Tristan, Texas, had drawn him back because that was where Ben Whyte had spent the majority of his miserable childhood. It was a rural area of southern Texas surrounded by nothing but flat arid land. Familiarity had drawn the man back.

He shook his head as he mulled over the details of the call. Ben Whyte hadn't had a chance. He'd come out of the ashes of an abusive childhood deeply scarred. It was urgent that he find Ava immediately. Ben Whyte was an unpredictable, troubled man. Not only that, but if what his mother said was true, like his father, he had no love of women. A woman-hating man with a grudge. He shuddered at the thought of it.

Thirty minutes later, Faisal had the chopper pilot drop him five miles from Tristan town limits. In a town this size, the arrival of a helicopter wasn't going to go unnoticed. He had a vehicle waiting for him. It was a basic silver SUV that blended in with all the others. It was the perfect choice—mass-produced, dull and mundane. It was exactly what he needed to remain under the radar. While the town was a good size, it was still small enough that a stranger would eventually be noticed by someone.

His mind went over all that had transpired. What did Ava think she was doing? She'd phoned for his help and now fled it. He'd considered possibilities including that somehow she might have had a heads-up on the man who had killed the patient after her. Hospital surveillance hadn't told him much more than that he was an average-sized male who had kept his face carefully hidden from the surveillance cameras. So far, he appeared to be working alone.

His phone buzzed. This time it was his contact within the Canadian RCMP, Sergeant Aaron Detrick. "There's a bit of information I thought you ought to know. I was just speaking to one of the other officers who had worked undercover on the case we discussed. Chan has a couple of go-to men, basically killers for hire he uses. It's not often. I think, rather ironically, like I said before, Chan considers himself a good guy."

"Some good guy," Faisal said, and then he regretted

the interjection. Aaron tended to be a bit long-winded if given any kind of encouragement.

"There's one name that came up just recently, Dallas Tenorson. He's been arrested a number of times. Violent acts, a brutal beating during a robbery, road rage, but nothing to keep him locked up for any length of time. Except, we were sure he was behind a killing last spring. Cause of death, gunshot to the head. One shot took the victim out cleanly—that doesn't happen often. It had hit man written all over it, between that and a clean crime scene. No one was ever convicted. The evidence was just too thin. But the interesting thing is that the man who died had been up on charges for rape. He raped Chan's daughter. She committed suicide immediately after the rape."

"A tragedy," Faisal said, thinking of the girl.

"Chan never missed a beat," Aaron said.

"He's tough," Faisal said with a hint of sarcasm.

"And more importantly smart, but he tripped up this time. We were able to ID the last hit man he used but we've got no evidence to pin on Darrell. We have suspicion based on recent activity and a witness who insists they'll commit suicide before they admit what they know on the record. So unofficially, like I said, his name is Dallas Tenorson. He's been in and out of juvie, is from a broken home—the classic story. His record from juvie has been purged so now there's no record, nothing to prevent him from moving freely around the country or across borders. He has a passport. Now thirty years old and has never held a steady job. So how is he surviving? Contract work, if you get my drift."

Faisal's laugh was dry. It wasn't a drift but a slam in the head. Everything he'd heard up until the hit man's description had been enough to make him sick. This Dallas—he deserved what he got. Up to no good and destroying other people's lives. Faisal wouldn't mind being the one to take him out. He pushed his thoughts aside. Instead he said, "I'm guessing that you've got nothing to pin him with."

"No evidence. We know he's transient and smart enough to cover his tracks. There was no paperwork found for the two previous hits, no electronic trail—phone trail, nothing. They had to have met in person but there's no witness either. We had a guy undercover, but he didn't get close enough to nail him, just close enough to make some pretty valid assumptions. Anyway, I'm telling you this so you can keep a watch out. I've sent you a picture too. Should be on your phone now. That's pretty much all I can do. Anything else and I'll be stepping over a line. Trouble with the law," he laughed. "Okay, it wasn't funny."

Faisal chuckled. "Not really, but thanks for the effort, man."

After Faisal disconnected, he wondered what else there might be. He knew he was lucky in his line of work to have established such a connection. He could only be grateful for what he got.

From everything he knew and from what Aaron had told him, he knew that time was running out.

Chan was on his way to Hong Kong and, if he followed his former pattern, being crossed, in this case defrauded, meant he'd put the pins in place. Someone was going to die and he'd bet that someone might be Ben Whyte. But with Ben potentially on Ava's trail, that left her in the middle.

He just hoped and prayed that he hadn't arrived too late.

Chapter Twenty

Faisal took a room in a run-down motel on the outskirts of town. That was where he began his search for Ava. As far as choice there wasn't any. It appeared that all the motels on the edge of town were run-down. But it was there that he'd be less noticed. It wasn't unlike other towns. The only exception was that Tristan was more worn—more forgotten.

Finding Ava was critical. Ben might be here too but his priority was making sure Ava was safe and literally out of the line of fire. He ached to see her but despite the small size of this town, it might not be that easy.

He was dressed down and the vehicle he'd rented was a few years old. And after the last few days running between searching the water and going to the hospital, his after-five shadow had turned into stubble. He was not unlike many of the scruffy men he'd seen in the nearby Flying J. Or the two men he'd seen enter the diner next door. If someone was going to remain unseen, the best thing to do was remain on the fringes. The people who didn't fit, and those that had secrets, congregated there. He'd seen these types of places again and again while working a variety of cases across the country. They were places where secrets could be hidden. Knowing that, it was the logical place to start. And it was really only a place to set up his home base. He doubted if he would be spending much time in this room. The best way to start searching for Ava was by questioning the people who lived here. Someone had seen her. Someone knew who she was and he'd find that someone if it took all night.

Ava. He'd never forgotten her and he knew now that he never would. He only hoped that he could find her, that she was safe, that if she were willing, he could hold her in his arms again.

But he'd no sooner dropped his small duffel bag on the worn double bed in the grim little room than a gunshot sounded outside blowing any of his hopes aside. He was on his feet and his Glock was in both hands. An engine revved. Glass crashed and someone shouted and then there was silence.

The silence didn't last long. It was soon filled with a woman's voice and a string of curses. Her shouts filled the parking lot. He pulled the ratty curtain back and could see a woman standing in the fading evening light with her hands on her hips only six feet to the right and in front of him. It looked to him like she was the aggressor. As such, she didn't appear to be in immediate danger. She hurled a bottle onto the pavement. Shards of green glass scattered in every direction and glinted under the light of a nearby parking lot. Ten or so feet away, a biker with black leather chaps and a faded red bandanna on his head shook his fist at her; in his left hand he held a handgun. He could guess now what had happened. There'd been a fight and now the gun was being used as a scare tactic, nothing more. Still, he didn't like it. The woman, no matter how worn out she looked or what her occupation, didn't deserve that kind of treatment.

Faisal opened the door to his room and stepped out. It was clear now, from the gestures of the biker as he left the lot, that the shot had only been meant to frighten and not harm. It was also clear that the woman, now that she had thrown the bottle, was unarmed. It had been the biker who had shot in the air.

"Ma'am, are you alright?"

The woman's eyes were wild, her hair in tangles. She was wearing a faded yellow wifebeater shirt. The cotton sagged and her dark nipples were clear against the thin fabric. *Wife beater.* He grimaced. But as much as he hated the term for the sleeveless T-shirt, here it seemed troublingly appropriate. But despite her revealing and worn-out attire, her legs were positioned in a fighting stance. Her hands were in fists and her arms were rigid at her side.

Oblivious to his words, she told him where to go in words he had no respect for.

The woman turned her attention to him. "I'm not

interested in you either. No man is getting anything free. You want…"

"No." He cut her off. "I'm not interested."

"Not good enough for you, boy?" she asked. Her double chin quivered and her brow wrinkled. She ran a hand through her hair, which was platinum blond with mud-brown roots.

"You're beautiful, ma'am," he said. Flattery was a powerful tool to manipulate people. He thought that maybe she deserved a compliment—he doubted if she got any from the looks of her and this place. This area, this hotel, all of it, didn't attract the kind of people who were into niceties.

"You'll do," she said with a smile. "Flattery and chivalry will get you everywhere," she said in a tone and with words that hinted at more sophistication than the earlier incident and her appearance indicated.

He held his phone out to her with a picture of Ava. "Have you seen this woman?"

She paused. "Yeah," she said thoughtfully, chewing her bottom lip. "She was here this morning, asking for work. I run this joint in case you're asking. Not that it's much." She shook her head. "Anyway, as far as rooms, we've got none but the Blue Moon down the road does. I told her to go there." She looked at him with more street wisdom than real smarts. "For a fifty I'll give you a bit more." Her eyes roved over him.

Faisal couldn't help himself, he gave her the fifty. "Treat yourself," he said gruffly. He hoped if nothing else, the money would keep her off her back and give her some dignity, at least for one night.

He turned and headed for the SUV. He needed to get to the Blue Moon and he needed to do it, like, yesterday.

Ava was exhausted. She'd gone from a hospital bed to cleaning rooms in the space of less than two days. The evening sun had just set as Ava turned out the light and slipped into bed. Despite being physically drained, it was still early and she couldn't sleep. Instead, she was plagued by thoughts and possibilities. She'd learned that land transactions were not immediately filed online in Tristan if at all. In the land registry's dismal and tiny office, the woman in charge was good-natured and after paying the fee she requested, was more than willing to give her a photocopy of the deed and transfer documents for the land her father had told her about that fateful night on the yacht. In fact, she'd given her copies of two land transfers— the second had come as a surprise but it too had her father's forged signature.

Now she had the evidence that at least the signature on the piece of land in question that Ben Whyte was selling wasn't her father's. Tomorrow she'd turn what she had over to the authorities. Today wasn't an option as the county sheriff's office was in the next town and she wasn't sure if she wanted to hand this over to the local police office which consisted of two officers. When she'd asked the librarian about them she'd been given a lackluster review.

She hated being here, hated everything about this place. The sooner she could deliver what she'd found to the authorities, the sooner she could get out of here. She didn't feel safe here, not in this shoebox of a room, not in this town. Her breath came in on a hitch as she thought of Faisal.

She could hear his voice like he was here, low, deep and confident. She remembered how he'd told her that she was safe when she'd been in the hospital. And she'd felt safe not because of where she was but because he'd been there. She never should have left him or tried to do this on her own. Now she longed to hear his voice. She needed him and yet she'd run from the help he'd offered. She'd done the right thing, she reassured herself. As much as she longed for him, this was on her.

She lay on her back, staring at the ceiling. Too tired to get up and too distracted with her whirling thoughts to sleep. A car pulled up. She tensed. Instinct told her to leave the light off, as if she sensed something wrong. There was a knock on the room to her right and then silence. There was no one there. That room was empty.

Who did they want?

Who were they looking for?

She felt like a kid holding her breath at the scary part of a movie. Instead of holding her breath she was remaining still, quiet, listening.

The footsteps crunched on the gravel. That meant they were coming closer. It was a strange fact she'd noted on arrival, that the end units had gravel stalls while the rest of the parking lot was paved. It was like the pavers had run out or became exhausted by the project before completion. Either way, she'd seen it as an odd little bonus. It made detecting someone nearby, especially in a vehicle, somewhat easier.

She sat up, swinging her feet to the ground, thankful that she'd slept in her T-shirt and scrub pants.

She couldn't stand another minute without finding out who was there. But when she peeked out the peephole, there was nothing. The peephole had a limited range though. She took a step back. Her heart pounded as if instinct was again telling her what her other senses couldn't, that something was wrong.

A bang on the edge of the parking lot, as if someone had hit a metal pole with a large heavy object, had her biting back a shriek and jumping away from the door. Could it be gunfire? But that was insane— or was it? She remembered her employer mentioning something about a nearby gun range. That explained it. A sigh of relief raced through her. But she had to make certain. She pulled the faded blue cotton curtain back a few inches and peeked out. She could see nothing, the lighting was too weak. She thought of her exit strategy. If there was a problem, the front was already compromised. The bathroom window was small but she could fit; she'd already checked out that option.

There wasn't a threat, she told herself through gritted teeth. *Relax.*

She squinted as if that would allow her to see more than what the filmy light of the one parking lot light and her outside unit light allowed. The parking lot was half-empty but the motel was only half-full. It turned out that had worked in her favor, for she'd only had to work a partial shift to finish up what another employee hadn't. Physically, she couldn't have done more. Traveling here had taken what little energy she had.

The motel sign sent a thin bluish stream of light across the parking lot, from the north side. Nothing moved. She took a deep breath and let the curtain drop. Then she retreated to the bed, where she perched as if she might need to leap up and run.

Seconds and then minutes ticked by.

She began to relax when she heard footsteps again. Again, they seemed close to her room. Then they stopped. Somehow the silence was more frightening. Again, she moved to the window, glanced sideways and crouched down, peering over the window ledge. What she saw frightened her. A man stood in the faint light. He was maybe fifteen feet from her front door. A car door banged. His back was to her, facing the parking lot before he moved away deeper into the lot. Then he turned. She knew that profile, that large, rather hooked nose was distinctive. The light outlined him perfectly.

Ben Whyte.

Her mouth went dry and her hand shook as she

dropped the curtain. Did he know she was here? In this room? Had he discovered that Anne Brown was Ava Adams?

She stood up. She looked at what stood between her and danger: a weak safety chain, an economy lock and a cheap flimsy door. Again, she crouched down, trying to keep out of sight. She nervously lifted the curtain, an inch, then two. She peeked out the window. Now she could see the shadow of what looked like a man crouched low and moving from the fringes of the parking lot directly toward her. He was coming in at a different angle, not walking upright as if he had honest business but rather as if he was sneaking in. Whoever he was, this was someone different.

Her heart raced and her mouth was dry. None of this boded well. She hadn't been comfortable from the beginning and had slept in her clothes as if prepared to run. Now her fear had been validated.

She backed up and spun around, heading for the bathroom where the small window led to the back alley.

She needed to get out fast while she still had the chance.

Chapter Twenty-One

Faisal had stopped in the office of the Blue Moon Hotel. The office was separate from the row of units that sat diagonally from it. He'd walked in from the street, not wanting to call attention to himself or alert anyone to his presence.

He walked into the office prepared to face whoever was manning this operation with all the charm he could muster. A woman lifted her head from the desk, looked at him with rheumy dark eyes and smiled. Her disheveled bleached blond hair was giving him déjà vu, for it reminded him of the manager's style in the hotel he had checked into. He pushed that thought aside. He needed information and he needed to concentrate to get it.

"Can I help you?"

Her round, out-of-shape body leaned over the counter, spilling her large breasts literally onto the counter. He kept his eyes on her face, ignored her disappointed look and smiled his most charming smile.

"Beautiful night," he said.

"It is."

And from there he turned on the charm. It was a gift that he rarely used but one that came naturally. Ironically, he'd used it twice in the space of an hour. He gave his full attention to the woman on the other side of the counter. By the time he was done with his "feel good," "you're the greatest" routine, he'd asked the questions he needed to and gotten the answer to each of them. She readily identified Ava from a picture.

"She checked in this morning. Poor thing needed work. She covered an afternoon shift," she said, her eyes roving over him. "She's in the end unit."

He left the office with a smile and a quick salute and headed away from the units she'd pointed at. He'd seen movement he couldn't identity, and putting himself into a possible line of fire was no way to help Ava.

He moved quietly along the fringes of the parking lot of the Blue Moon Motel. It was dark and there was no traffic on the road that skirted the motel that he now knew Ava was staying at. He crouched down using the darkness as cover. He paused for a moment to take stock of the situation. He gave himself a minute and then two, for he was hidden behind a boulder that looked like it had been placed there in an aborted attempt at landscaping. Ahead, the lot was dimly lit by a light on one side and the blue light that thinly streamed from the motel sign. The place was run-down, the motel itself painted a faded and dismal gray. Ironically, that fact was at complete odds with what one might expect given the motel's name—Blue Moon Motel. The only thing blue was the annoying sign that cast blue tendrils of light across everything.

His attention turned toward the movement he saw by the end unit. It was the bulky shadow of a man. He had a picture on his phone, thanks to his RCMP contact, of the hit man but in the muted light from this distance, he wasn't identifying anything. A shadow moved farther away. The bulk indicated it might be another man. The first man was nearer the building, while the other man was yards away, putting him on the edge of the parking lot. A gunshot echoed through the night and he hit the ground near the sidewalk, where he immediately rose to his haunches and moved behind the hood of the nearest vehicle.

Dallas Tenorson or Ben Whyte or both could be here or not and it was all supposition. The only thing that was for sure was that a gun had been fired. He was pretty sure it had been from the man nearer the motel units aiming for a second one in the parking lot. But the man at the fringes had not fired back. That in itself was an interesting fact.

The information he'd received confirmed that Ben Whyte was in the area. Could one of the two be Ben? If it was Ben, he had the home advantage. These were his childhood stomping grounds. He knew every bit of this land. He'd known that the land deals had been nothing but worthless contracts. He'd known it all, for this was where they'd been inked. It was here that they had fleeced enough buyers to make Ben a rich man if he could just cash in on his last deal.

He crouched down. He had his gun out and in one hand. He wasn't expecting to shoot anyone, not yet. He hoped not ever, but then he always hoped that. He squinted. He could see the shadowy figures, one moving in on the other. He wasn't sure what was going on. His priority was keeping Ava safe, and to do that he needed to get her out of there as quickly as possible.

One man moved closer to her door. Too close for his liking. He knew who it must be. He could see the off-kilter way he walked, as if one leg couldn't quite support the weight that was expected of it. He knew why he walked that way. One of the unit lights near the end clicked on and then immediately off but it was enough to see the distinctive profile that was Ben Whyte.

Faisal shifted his Glock, feeling the comforting weight. He had no sympathy for either Dallas Tenorson, a man who seemed to spend his life contracting to kill, or Ben Whyte, his intended victim. If the second man was Dallas, then there was no way he could take him out without giving an open path for Ben to kill Ava. Ava's room remained in darkness and he could only wonder if she was awake or asleep. Was she spooked by the earlier gunfire? There was always the chance that she'd open the door and make herself vulnerable. He could try to take at least one of these men out but neither were close enough for a clean shot.

It was too dangerous. He couldn't risk trying to

take either of them out and alerting the other to his presence. Instead, he had to sneak around them and get Ava out before he addressed the other two. To do that he was going to have to go around back. He could only hope that, like every motel built in this style, there was a window in the bathroom. He thought of fire codes. He didn't know what the damn fire codes were—he could only pray. If there wasn't a window... The thought dropped. He wouldn't think of that and would just have come up with a new plan then if it came to that. He began to make his way around the building, moving quickly before the explosive situation in front of him blew up.

A movement ahead. Ben Whyte was five yards from Ava's front door. There was no more time to consider. He had to move. He ducked down behind a worn-out van with chipped gray paint. Another shot was fired and the man on the fringes of the worn parking lot dropped. The shot was masked by the sound of a semi pulling out on the edges of the commercial district of town.

He couldn't get a clear shot from here. With his gun in both hands he moved quickly and quietly to the back of the building. He slipped around the building with his back to the wall, watching for movement in the darkness broken only by a yard light over fifty feet away.

Two minutes later he was outside Ava's back window. He gave the signal that they'd used so often, what seemed like forever ago. He waited. Nothing.

He tapped on the window again. One, two, three—same as he had so many years ago when he called her out in their university days to whatever party had been going on. He hoped she remembered. Hoped that she realized the danger and got out before it was too late. Before he needed to do something more drastic that could compound the danger she was already in.

She had to remember. But he couldn't assume anything, couldn't make that mistake, for Ava's life was on the line.

Chapter Twenty-Two

Someone or something was tapping on the bathroom window. Ava bit back a shriek. She was blocked in. She'd heard what sounded like a gunshot in the parking lot and she'd kept low after that, afraid to look out or to somehow draw attention to herself. Now there was someone at the back—her only escape hatch. Her tiny sanctuary had just become her trap. Her heart pounded and she was glad she hadn't had a chance to eat much or she was sure fear would have her heaving it all. She was poised in the doorway of the bathroom to run and there was nowhere to run to.

She couldn't breathe and her heart was racing.

That familiar tap again. The tap that had meant so many other things so long ago. Was it her imagination? Wishful thinking? Or divine providence? It didn't matter if it was none or any of them. She had no choice. She had to take the chance. It could be anyone or it could be him.

She didn't need any other motivation. She didn't care who was in the alley. Fear skated over everything her rational mind told her, and she knew that she had to get out.

Her hands shook as she balanced on the tub. She pushed but the window seemed stuck. She pushed again. Her nail ripped. She didn't stop. Finally, the window opened a crack and with a heave she pushed it all the way up. The faded, blue-checked curtain fell across her face and she pushed it aside as she boosted herself up. Fortunately, the window was big enough that she was easily able to slip out of it without bodily contortions. She dropped to the ground just as she heard the crack of wood splitting and knew that the door to her room had just burst open.

She landed hard and stumbled. She reached out as if intuitively she'd known all along that someone friendly was here, someone who would stop her from stumbling or face planting. That was only wishful thinking. She had to get out of here if she wanted to live.

"It's me."

A man. Her heart was pounding so hard that she thought her chest would burst.

She bit back a scream, backed up and turned to run. She'd give it her best. She wouldn't die from lack of trying. Instead she ran straight into the solid wall of a chest and strong arms that held her tight. There was no escape. She was doomed and if it weren't for the arms holding her, she was sure she might have expired from fright.

She tried to twist away and at the same time she tried to make herself smaller, to slip out of the iron grip that held her. Her heart was beating so fast and so loud that she thought she might die just from that alone. Fear raced through her and at the same time anger was building. The adrenaline rush was more from anger than fear now. She'd live through this or die trying. She raised her foot to bring it down on the beige canvas high-top sneaker. *Not an ordinary shoe. Designer.* The words ran through her mind but didn't connect with what that meant.

"Ava."

She twisted and managed to sink her teeth into his hand. A curse and then she was turned roughly around to face him.

"Damn it."

The grip loosened and she was free. But the freedom only lasted a few seconds before he had her again. This time by her waist, her feet off the ground, she was held tight against him.

She kicked backward and clipped his shin.

"Ava, it's me... Faisal."

She hadn't heard right and yet she had. The voice, the words, even the shoes. It all came together. All of it was familiar. The fear fell away. She relaxed in his arms, her heart pounding a zillion miles an hour. The danger she had anticipated replaced by a danger that had a different meaning, different depth.

"Fai?" she said, even though the familiarity of the voice validated the truth.

"If I let you go, promise me you won't run," he said.

"I wouldn't—"

"I'd catch you anyway," he cut her off darkly.

"Let me go," she said. "I won't run." That part was true, for she had no vehicle and no place to run to. "But it's a mistake to be here with me."

His arm eased and she slid down his hard length, landing on her feet, as she turned to face him.

The look he gave her was both intimidating and full of concern. "You could have died, running the way you did."

"But I didn't," she said obstinately, as if her earlier fears had been based on nothing but her imagination. "It was a mistake to follow me," she repeated, for he hadn't responded the first time she'd said it. "Fai," she whispered. "You need to get out of here. Trust me."

"We'll get out of here together. This is what I do—protect."

"I know," she whispered but she really wasn't quite sure she did. She knew about his company, even knew about his position but she'd never imagined any of this. She wasn't sure any layperson actually could.

"It's dangerous," she said as if he'd said nothing at all. "Being with me."

"I can take care of myself, Ava, and you. You need me. Maybe more than you realize."

Something deep inside told her that he was right. That it had been a mistake to come here alone. "There's someone after me. He'll kill—"

"Let's get you out of here. This place has been compromised."

A gunshot seared the night and overrode the other sounds. She bit back a scream.

"Damn it."

He grabbed her hand without another word. They were running down the narrow overgrown alley, where trees grew wild and uncontrolled by a gardener's clippers. Their branches reaching beyond the confines of the yards they grew in, crowding the alley. He boosted her over a fence, through a yard cluttered with aged vehicles. A dog barked. The sound muffled and slightly ominous as if there was something the dog could see and they couldn't.

She ran as if he were her only salvation. And she supposed it was true. She'd be dead if Faisal hadn't been here. Her father had died and she knew that she was next on the list. She clung tighter to his hand and wished she could go back to a place in time when she'd never run from him in the first place. She couldn't protect him. It had been foolish of her to try.

BEN COULDN'T BELIEVE IT. Darrell Chan had tried to take him out.

Despite the advice he'd given Chan, despite how convincing he'd believed he'd been, Chan hadn't listened. He'd told Chan that purchasing land in this area would be slow going. Tristan wasn't a big place and the land-registry process moved like everything else—slowly. He'd told Chan that it was best not to delay paying the purchase price since that would grease the system's wheels and get everything moving faster. Apparently, Chan hadn't believed him, about anything. The deal had fallen through.

He ducked behind a car and could see the man Chan had sent after him was still moving. He'd thought he'd gotten him minutes ago and had gone for the little witch in the interim. That had been a mistake. He rubbed his shoulder. He'd almost got it then.

He narrowed his eyes, watching. He knew who he was up against. He'd done his research. The loser was a hired killer. Chan had used him before; he was good. But he wasn't that good.

Ben moved diagonally. He was in the open but he was low and it was dark. A shot hit close enough to kick up dirt and make a pebble clip his wrist. He bit back a curse and put his mouth on the wound.

Damn it, he thought with a snarl. He flattened himself to the ground by the back tire of a van and watched, waiting. The loser had taken his last shot. He'd picked the wrong man to try to take out. He hadn't spent hours at the range for nothing. This guy was done.

He dropped to his chest as he had a brief visual and then nothing. He inched forward, both hands on his gun, his eyes combing the half-empty lot, searching for him. The one who saw the other first was the one who would come out of here alive.

There'd be one more shot.

It would be his.

Movement.

Running. The slap of sneakers on pavement. A shadow of a man.

He took aim and fired. Once, twice.

Someone would hear him.
Damn it. He didn't care. He shot again.
His target fell.
It was time to get the hell out of here.

Chapter Twenty-Three

"How did you find me?" Ava gasped as she was literally dragged by her hand. She knew that Faisal was pacing himself, that he was holding back. She was running full tilt, giving it her all. But she was no runner. She needed to stop for breath. "Those were gunshots?" she gasped. "What's going on?"

"Keep moving," he gritted. They'd already jumped one broken fence. Now, he was almost lifting her over another listing three-foot fence that backed yet another property.

There was no time to answer anything. They needed to get out of the area. They ran for a few more minutes, taking them another block away before he stopped.

"You're alright?"

"I need to rest," she gasped.

She looked at Faisal and saw that he had a gun in his hand. The sight of that did nothing for her pounding heart. This was unbelievable, unthinkable. She'd known Faisal's work could be dangerous but somehow she'd never imagined this. She couldn't fathom it. Instead, she looked around. The street they were on seemed quiet, deserted. Across the street was a steel Quonset and she remembered another time and something else her father had said.

"You're remembering," Faisal said as his dark eyes scanned her face.

She nodded. "My memory is back."

"Can you go any farther?" he asked. "You can tell me everything later. And I can tell you what you need to know, what I've found out."

"He wants to kill me."

"I know," he interrupted. "But someone's been sent to take him out. I don't know which of them is going to walk out of that parking lot. But we're going to be as far away as possible."

"This is beyond what I thought."

"Way beyond."

"What else do you know?" she asked.

"More than you think," he replied. "But right now I need to get you to safety."

FIVE MINUTES LATER Faisal had left Ava in the driver's seat of the SUV he'd rented. He'd made sure all the doors were locked. And he'd given her strict instructions that if anyone but he approached the vehicle, she should take off and never look back. He didn't think that would happen. Where she was, in the parking lot of a local fast-food restaurant, couldn't be any more well-lit and, therefore, any safer. "If you feel threatened in any way, drive. Don't analyze it, just go. Head for Ballad," he said mentioning the next town twenty miles west of Tristan where the sheriff's office was located. "Promise me you won't hesitate. You'll just go and report everything to the sheriff there."

"I promise," she said.

He'd left her there. It was the best place he could come up with in a time crunch. He had to go back. He'd run all the way back, daily sprints making the run easy. Five minutes later, he stood on the fringes of the parking lot outside the motel room that Ava had called home for not quite a day. A man lay sprawled on his back ten feet from the lone parking lot light. Otherwise, the lot was empty of people and dotted with the same vehicles that had been there fifteen minutes ago.

He moved carefully forward, crouched down to approach the body. He assumed it wasn't Ben. He needed to be sure. The body was lying faceup. He beamed a small flashlight at the figure that was obviously dead. The man matched the picture of Dallas Tenorson. Wiry, early thirties, dark hair and he guessed about five foot eight. He went through the man's pockets. No identification but he didn't expect any. The hit man had come to take Ben Whyte out and instead Ben had taken him. He didn't feel anything for him. These types of men were desperate, dangerous, from hard backgrounds, and they lived and died by violence. To them, a life was only as good as the coin you could lay on it.

He moved silently across the parking lot, keeping

low and out of sight. He could see the flicker of a television through the window in one room. He thought of the gunshots, not many admittedly but still enough to have attracted attention. A dead man in the parking lot to cap everything and still it had brought no curious bystanders from their units. Everyone was caught in their own melodrama whether real or spoon-fed to them through the television screen. Beyond them was undeveloped land and a shooting range. You couldn't have picked a better place to take someone out. Ava had set herself up perfectly without even realizing it. But then how could she have known? The shooting range was hidden. It was behind the dilapidated warehouse that sat diagonally across from a commercial lot. He'd seen it himself only because he'd driven a back road in that took him past the facility. So gunshots wouldn't be unexpected in this rough area near a shooting range. It was a shooter's nirvana.

Five yards from Ava's room he could see that the gravel had been disturbed with what looked like a footprint. He thought of the dead man. The same fate could have befallen Ava if he hadn't been there. The thought of it made him sick. The door was cracked and he only had to push gently for it to open. Inside, the bed cover had been thrown across the room and there were towels scattered on the floor as if they'd been thrown in frustration. There was nothing else, no personal belongings, nothing left behind to give any indication as to who had been here.

On a hunch, he lifted the mattress and there was an

envelope. He picked it up and looked inside, quickly thumbing through the papers and seeing that they pertained to land transactions. Ava had been busy.

He stepped back outside where he made a call to the local authorities and asked for the chief of the local police department. Davis O'Connor was a man he'd contacted earlier. He liked to be prepared for such things. You never knew when you might need police assistance, especially in his field. He had been proactive this time too and had made sure that the law knew who he was, but not precisely what he was about.

Now they had a murder and he knew they wouldn't be returning to Miami, at least not immediately. There was the hurricane warning affecting flights into the area. But more importantly, this had to be reported. It was pretty much a given that the police would want them to hang around. A fair enough request as long as he could keep Ava safe.

He'd thought this was a targeted hit. It was about Ava. He hadn't expected what he found when he entered the main office. There, the same woman who had eaten up all the charm he could throw at her now lay in front of the check-in counter on her back, a bullet hole in her chest, blood covering her blouse. Her eyes were open and she looked rather surprised. He squatted down. He knew what the outcome was before he did it—he took her pulse anyway.

"Sweet hell," he muttered as he strode out of the office.

Faisal could hear the sirens now. He jogged back

to get Ava. The police would want to speak to her too. He slipped into the passenger seat leaving her in the driver's seat. He put a hand over hers as she reached as if to turn the key and start the vehicle. Her bottom lip quivered and he moved closer putting his arm over her shoulder, offering her comfort with his touch and protection always.

"You came back for a reason, Ava. What was it?" he asked softly.

"Dad told me to read his emails and I did when I got here to Tristan. Darrell Chan said that he had proof that Dad had sold him land, that his name was on documents he had in hand. Dad claimed he'd never made such a transaction."

"Your father had no interest in real estate but his name carries a lot of weight."

"Exactly," she interrupted. "But Chan had documents with Dad's signature on them. Dad told me the proof of his innocence was here, in Tristan."

"He told you to come here?"

She looked rather sheepish. "No. He told me to tell you."

"And you didn't." Anger ran through him at how she'd endangered herself.

"I'm sorry, Fai." Her voice trembled. Then she straightened her shoulders and turned to look at him. "But I found the proof to clear his name. The signatures on the transactions filed in Tristan are forged. I know Dad's signature. I need to go back and get the evidence."

He shook his head. "Is this it?" he interrupted her as he pulled out the envelope he'd taken from her hotel room.

"Yes. They're copies of both land transactions that Ben filed with forgeries of my father's signature. The last one was what was going to make Ben Whyte rich."

"And where Darrell Chan balked."

"Yes," she murmured. "Dad planned to come here and collect the evidence himself but if he couldn't, if something happened, he wanted me to tell the authorities or you what had happened and where the proof was. That's what he told me before the argument, before…" Her voice broke.

"Ava," he said, his eyes never leaving hers.

"I'm okay," she said. "Ben didn't know that my father was onto him. He arrived unexpectedly that night on the yacht, I'm not sure why."

"And your father somehow revealed what he knew or more likely Ben guessed," Faisal said. "Ben probably didn't know that Chan had already contacted your father."

She shook her head. "No and Dad didn't tell him, not then. Not while I was around."

"From what I can see, this land doesn't even belong to Ben or your father," Faisal said. "It was a fake transaction from start to finish."

"Unbelievable." She shook her head. "I think my father confronted Ben that night. A stupid move on his part," she said with sadness laced through the words.

"FAISAL AL-NASSAR?" The sheriff's deputy called out fifteen minutes later as he approached the motel office which the local police had now cordoned off with yellow tape.

"Yes. That's me," he said, coming forward with his arm outstretched. They shared a firm shake. Ava was at his elbow like a silent shadow.

"Hell of a mess. We're not used to murder in this town," Davis said as he came up beside the deputy a few minutes later. There was something that sounded like strain in his voice.

Faisal had told the deputy what he knew only minutes ago and Ava had added what she'd heard along with what she had found at the land registry office.

"We'll be interviewing the other guests, seeing if anyone saw anything." Davis tipped his cap. "You say that one was a hit man?"

"Yes." He gave him Aaron Detrick's number. "He has the information on that. I know if there's any way for them to pin something on their suspect they'll be more than grateful to you."

"RCMP you say. Be a first—never worked with a foreign government," Davis said with an off-kilter smile.

Faisal almost smiled at that. He doubted if he'd be working much with one now. If the case crossed borders it would be more than the police in this little town would see but rather the county sheriff, who had already stepped in, would be involved.

The police officer's phone rang and he walked

away to take the call while the deputy had moved on to examine other evidence. Two minutes later, Davis came over to where Faisal stood beside Ava. Her arm brushed his side as if touching him somehow gave her some solace.

"There was a sighting of a middle-aged man matching the description of this Ben Whyte just five miles outside of town. He was heading north." He looked at Ava. "The sheriff's office is on that. I think based on that, you're more than likely safe. Let me know what hotel you change to but stick here in Tristan. That's an order." He looked at Faisal. "Barring an emergency, I'll need you around for at least the next twenty-four hours." He shook Faisal's hand. He'd offered him a different level of respect than he would any other witness as soon as he'd learned of Faisal's connection to Nassar Security.

But no matter what had transpired, the truth was that Ben Whyte was still on the loose and Faisal wasn't so sure that he'd accomplished what he'd set out to do. Factoring out the manager of the motel who had been an unfortunate casualty, one man had died as he'd tried to take out another. Ben Whyte had lived. He'd been just outside Ava's motel room when Faisal had removed her from danger. The one thing that was clear was that Ben Whyte's work wasn't finished and that meant only one thing. He'd be back.

Chapter Twenty-Four

"Fai," Ava murmured.

She insisted on calling him by that abbreviated version of his name, one that only some of those closest to him used. Every time she did, it was like she had touched him with the heat of a lover's hand. It was outrageous, ridiculous. And he wanted to tell her to stop calling him that as much as he wanted her to call him that every day of his life. Few, except his brothers, called him by that name. He seemed swamped with nostalgia as he drove. He remembered the first time he had met her. He'd been enthralled with her. He would have dated her if he hadn't liked her so much, and if he hadn't been dating someone else. There were so many *if*s. None of his romantic entanglements at that time had turned out well. He didn't want to wreck a good friendship. That's what he'd told himself then. But the truth was that she slightly intimidated him with her drive to succeed. He'd never met anyone like her. And at the time, he'd been too young to appreciate her maturity. That combined with her drive gave her that edge. It was an edge that, for a young man, had been frightening. And he'd have died before he'd have admitted he was frightened of anything. That had been a long time ago. His thoughts shifted.

Two people had died, a man and a woman. He was used to it. She wasn't.

"You're alright?"

"Fine," she replied with a failed attempt at a smile. "At least I will be given time."

He knew that. If anyone, any layperson, could come back from this, it was Ava. The thought dropped. Thirty minutes later they stopped at a gas station with a small grocery and picked up a few things to have a casual meal. They had ready-made sandwiches and potato salad along with disposable plates and cutlery.

"Is that your stomach I hear?" Faisal asked. They had just settled into their new room in another place. It was an end room on the first floor of a hotel on the other side of town. He was putting potato salad on paper plates. The small counter was crowded with a coffeemaker and a microwave, leaving little space to work. He banged his hand once on the coffeemaker almost sending the carafe flying. He picked up the bottle of juice he'd bought from the motel vending machine and poured them each a glass. He took a plate and a glass over to her.

"Thanks," she said with a smile.

He made a second trip to get his own sandwich and drink. He made himself comfortable in the only other place to sit besides the two beds—an overstuffed, yet harder-than-rock faux leather chair.

She looked at him, her bare foot tucked under her legs as she stretched out on one of two twin beds. Her smile was contagious, whimsical and yet amused— a sign that even amid trouble and tragedy, life would eventually go on.

She took a bite of the sandwich. "Heaven," she said with a smile.

It dawned on him as he saw the slight shake of her hand and the ravenous way she bit into the sandwich that she hadn't eaten recently. "When was the last time you ate something that was cooked?"

"Something that wasn't peanut butter—is that what you mean?" she asked. "There wasn't any time to get groceries or, more accurately, I was too tired to hunt for anything better," she said before he could reply. She shook her head with a wry smile. "I guess that the last time, factoring out hospital food—" she grimaced "—was that night on the yacht."

"Ava, I'm sorry. And you've got nothing more than another sandwich, I'll—"

"No." She stopped him. "This is all I need for now. Promise me a good breakfast tomorrow and everything will be fine."

"Deal," he said with a laugh that was more expectation than amusement.

They ate in silence for a minute.

He finished his sandwich and came over to sit on the corner of the bed near her. She didn't look at him but instead wiped her mouth with a napkin. The sandwich had been thick with roast beef, lettuce and mayonnaise. A dab of mayonnaise was still on the upper corner of her mouth. He wiped it gently away. "I wish I could say that I won't ask you any more questions, knowing how much they upset you. But unfortunately—"

"You have no choice," she interrupted. "Don't feel bad. It needs to be discussed, figured out. Dad's name needs to be cleared. His name was used to steal millions of dollars and if he hadn't stumbled on the plot, it would have been much more. Ben Whyte used his good nature, convinced him he was helping a friend and then took advantage of him. First it was just financial support but then he forged his signature on land deeds. He was selling land that he didn't own and using my father's reputation to validate himself."

She was standing now, pacing.

He got up, taking her hands in his. "Ava. I'm so sorry you had to go through any of this."

"It's almost over, isn't it?"

"It is," he assured her.

She looked at him with wide, troubled eyes. "I missed you, Fai," she murmured.

"Why did you run? You know I would have protected you."

She shook her head. "I'm sorry. I didn't want you hurt, I…" Her gaze traveled to his waist where his Glock was holstered. "I should have known better. I regretted it later. If I could undo…"

"You doubted me?"

"Never... I..." She shook her head. "I don't know what I was thinking."

"It was a stupid mistake, sweetheart."

"Sweetheart," she repeated and looked up at him with a troubled frown.

"Promise me you'll never do that again."

"I hope I never am in such a situation, ever," she said instead.

"You won't be," he said grimly, his hands settling on her shoulders as he drew her closer. "I'll protect you always, Ava," he said in a low growl as his head bent and his lips met hers. At first the kiss was soft and hesitant, then it deepened and his tongue teased her lips to open. She felt so soft and vulnerable as he held her but he knew that was an illusion. He'd seen her strength. She'd proved it before and in spades these last few days. She was everything he'd ever imagined and more.

His phone rang.

He held her tighter.

The phone rang again and he reluctantly let her go.

"I'm sorry," he said after he'd seen the number display. "I need to take this. I'll be just outside."

"I think I'll run a shower," she said looking slightly bemused.

He wasn't sure what his brother Talib was calling about, but it would be something important. His timing couldn't have been worse.

He opened the door and stepped outside. The parking lot was dimly lit, similar to that of the Blue Moon Motel. He supposed it was a way of saving money. They weren't making a lot based on the price of the rooms. The Blue Moon. The comparison was like a warning running uncomfortably through him.

"Faisal?"

What Talib said next had his full attention.

"Coast Guard just reported in. They've found a Caucasian male on a yacht. He was found by an American container ship. The yacht drifted into the shipping lane. The man is alive but unconscious. They haven't made an identification yet, but…"

"There's a good chance it might be Dan Adams," Faisal said with a note of relief. "The IMO number matches," he said referring to the International Maritime Organization number on a boat's hull that identified it for the lifetime of the craft. "I'll keep it quiet until we have something for sure. There's no point in getting Ava's hopes up."

"She thinks he's dead?" Talib asked the question, which was more of a statement.

"Yeah. I haven't dissuaded her. There's too much at risk. Ben Whyte is still on the loose, and only four hours ago, the manager of the motel Ava had checked into was killed, as was Dallas Tenorson. He was hired to take out Ben Whyte."

"Bugger," Talib muttered. "This case is one ball of ugly."

"We're wrapping it up," Faisal said. "If the survivor turns out to be Dan, that will just be the icing on the cake. In the meantime, once the police have investigated and the weather improves on the east coast, we'll be moving on, heading back to Miami. We're hanging here in case we can provide the police with any more information. Ava's memory is back. I hope that what she remembers fills in any remaining gaps we have.

"Evidence points to the fact that Ben Whyte double-crossed the wrong man." He went on to explain to Talib what had happened earlier in the Blue Moon parking lot.

There were still questions. After he hung up with Faisal he strode the length of the lot. He stood there for a minute, breathing as if fresh air alone would give him the answers he needed. His mind went back to Darrell Chan. They knew that he was in Hong Kong at the moment. But they also knew that he had the resources to reach anyone he wanted anywhere in the world. The question was if he had the motive to do so. From what they'd gathered he did. Ben Whyte was still alive. It was only a matter of time before Darrell Chan hired someone else to take him out. That is if he hadn't already.

He headed back to the room but stopped when he saw that the door was open. He'd closed the door but he hadn't locked it. He'd been right outside, there had been no need to lock it. He should have locked the damn door.

There was a scuffling noise inside and then a small gasp. He'd recognize that voice anywhere—Ava.

He pushed open the door without hesitation. He

used the element of surprise as his gun was already in both hands, ready for use.

"What the hell?" Faisal stopped dead at the sight in front of him. Ava was being dragged backward by the sinewy tanned arm of a man who had a gun to her head.

"Come any closer and she dies."

"There's no need for this," Faisal said calmly as he watched Ben Whyte and prepared himself for any unexpected moves. The man didn't know him and yet he wasn't asking who he was. That didn't bode well.

"I thought I could just kill her and end this, but that's not true anymore is it?" Ben snarled.

"If this is about money, I can give you what you want and more."

Ben cursed, dropping one expletive after another. "Liar. You don't think I know that you want me dead."

"I'm not lying. I can get you out of the country a rich man. That's what you want, isn't it?" The words were difficult to say when what he really wanted to do was launch himself at the creep who held the woman he loved. The thought blazed through his mind without hesitation. It was overridden by his outrage over the situation she was in and his fear for her life. And, as a result, he skated right over the fact that a truth had again been laid bare if not in public, in his own heart.

Ben moved back, his grip on Ava's neck causing her to choke and clutch his arm with both hands as if she could pry the sinewy limb from her neck.

"I guarantee—a million dollars on the table. You

walk out of here a free man." He'd throw the damn money in a bag along with this piece of scum and drive him out of the country if necessary. At least that's what he'd tell him. In the end, he would drive him straight into the arms of the authorities and a jail cell, or kill him if necessary.

He deliberately tried to keep his eyes from Ava who had nothing but a towel around her. Her hair hung wet along her face and dripped down the towel. A long strand ran down the side of her neck. He pulled his attention away from her.

"I'm an Al-Nassar, we have…"

"I know who you are," Ben snarled. "Chan would have given me ten."

"I can easily do ten million," Faisal said as if this was nothing more serious than a game of poker.

He could feel his heart pounding. The stakes were higher than he could have imagined with Ava's life on the line. He was seriously making this up as he went along. He was using anything that was believable. Anything that would get Ava out of this man's arms and safe. That was all that mattered, and he'd say anything he needed to up until then.

He tried not to look at Ava, but it was difficult. She was right there. Looking frightened and courageous all at the same time. He wanted to tell her it would be alright, but he didn't know himself how this would turn out. There was still a good chance she could be injured or worse. He needed to play this right and play it well. And he didn't have much time to do it. It was a tight situation. He'd never been in any quite like it, at least not with someone he knew, someone he cared about. He forced his attention from Ava and to her captor. It was the only way.

Ben looked at Faisal in an odd way, the gun clenched in his hand, his grip on Ava's neck every bit as tight. But the expression on his face had changed. He was assessing Faisal now, slotting him into a different category.

Silence. Seconds ticked by.

"You're playing me," the man snarled. He took a step back, again roughly yanking Ava by the neck with him.

Ava bit her lip. A trickle of blood appeared, telling him how hard she was fighting for control. Her eyes met his as she tried to communicate with him. He could see fear and something else, something that told him that she was alright. They'd make it out of this, but he'd have to kill the bastard to do so. He just needed the opportunity. Her look told him everything he needed to know. She was in and on board. He had everything he needed except for a plan.

"Ben." It was time to get personal here. "The deal is brilliant."

"It is, isn't it?" This time his voice was captivated not by anything Faisal had said but instead, he suspected, by his own words. A narcissist at his worst, Faisal analyzed.

It was almost impossible not to look at Ava but he had to stay focused. He had an advantage; Ben's gun hand was wavering. His face was flushed. These were all signs that he was weakening. He could take him out. It would be risky, but he only needed one chance and he'd kill the no-good son of a desert dog. He wasn't sure if he could give Ava any kind of signal. He hoped she was following along, that she was on the same wavelength. He had to depend on that, on her wits.

A dog barked outside, distant, maybe a block away. Then a horn sounded and Ava jumped. It was all he needed. He had to take the chance. Otherwise, he knew deep in his gut that the outcome would be bad. He'd seen Ben's desperation. He knew the make-or-break of the situation and knew that with any more leeway, Ava was dead.

He gave her the look—subtle, just a flick of his gaze to his right. It was a signal to move where he indicated. Instead she stood there. She seemed paralyzed in place before sinking her teeth into Ben's hand. His grip loosened and she slipped away.

Faisal shot—aiming with all the skill the hours at the range had given him. Yet, all the while he wondered how things had come to this. To Ava standing, half-dressed, seemingly in shock. Her face white, her black hair long and wild, only the towel wrapped around her. He registered all that as he watched the man fall, as blood ran onto the floor and it was clear that whatever danger he presented was over.

Still, he needed to get her out of here. The dead man was too close to Ava. She'd survived the first trauma but the second was threatening to do her in. She was shaking. He pulled her tight against him, his arm over her shoulders, her head on his shoulder.

"It's over," he whispered into the faint rose scent of her hair. He felt her quiver against him. "Let's get out of here," he said, and this time he meant they were taking the chopper and getting the hell out of Texas. Sheriff's orders or not, they were out of here. He'd put in his report and then hit the road. The Lone Star state had offered enough challenge, for the time being anyway.

She looked up at him as if finally realizing what had happened as she looked at the body and her lips tightened.

"Is it over?"

"He's dead."

"He wanted to kill me," she murmured as she wiped tears away with the back of one hand.

"Ava..." he began, reaching to take her into his arms. To comfort her, to...

She pushed him gently back. "It's alright. I'm fine. I suppose we need to call the police—again." She drawled out the last bit.

"Again," he agreed. "This time I lay odds we'll be taken down to the station."

She smiled wanly at him. "It beats how I spent the last few minutes. I think we'll both survive."

"Let's get you away from this," he said.

"Let me get dressed," she said.

"I'll get your clothes," he said. There was no way he

was letting her step around the body to get her things in the bathroom. Instead he did it for her and stood with his back to her and between her and the corpse as she dressed.

A minute later she was dressed and ready to go. He had her hand and it felt like he would never let her go. And even while doing that, he was on the phone. The police needed to be informed.

"Do you think we'll ever know what happened to my father?" she asked softly.

Faisal looked at her as they leaned against the rental, waiting for the authorities. "I don't doubt it," he replied.

"I wish Dad had…" She choked, unable to finish her thoughts. And they both knew what that last word that she couldn't say was. She wished that her father had lived.

There was nothing he could say. He didn't want to offer her false hope. There was still a chance that her father hadn't survived. Everything was still too volatile. Chan was still on the loose and Dallas Tenorson might be dead but he was only one of a number of hit men Darrell Chan could have hired. This case wasn't closed yet, not by a long shot. Danger still lurked.

Chapter Twenty-Five

They had just finished giving their report at Tristan's police office where two deputies from the county sheriff's office had remained on site. Both Faisal and Ava had told the men what they knew. It was close to midnight before they were able to leave. Faisal opened the door of the SUV and Ava slipped in.

They'd just received the news from Talib that Darrell Chan was still in Hong Kong. On a tip from the RCMP, he was detained by Chinese authorities on conspiracy to commit murder. As well as a possible second-degree-murder charge. If everything went as planned, he'd be facing justice in either a Canadian or an American court. The authorities from the countries involved would be negotiating that. Whichever country's court he landed in, the odds were that he wouldn't be a free man for a very long time, if ever.

"It's odd… Darrell Chan was rather a silent criminal," Ava mused. "Not someone you'd fear on the street, but don't cross him. Dad would have appreciated…" She couldn't say any more; tears threatened.

He took her in his arms. "Ava," he murmured against the soft fragrance of her hair. There was nothing more to say, no certain news that would bring her comfort.

"Dad was taken advantage of," Ava said. "He was so mild-mannered."

"Which is what Ben counted on. He had a plane ticket for Thailand leaving in the next week. One way."

"Then why did he want my father…"

"He needed to convince his last client. Your father has a reputation of being aboveboard and honest. That information is easy to learn. He's a local celeb."

She considered that for a moment. "I never quite thought of it that way."

"If the deal with Chan had gone through, Ben would have had enough money to end his illicit career. This part of it is only a guess, but from what I'm getting from my Thai source, he'd already rented a property in northern Thailand for the next month using his grandmother's maiden name. What he planned to do after that is anyone's guess."

"What's yours?" Ava asked softly.

"He was going off the grid. Disappearing and living out his life. We more than likely wouldn't have heard from Ben Whyte again. But I don't think that means he'd stop. Con artists are a strange bunch."

"They're proud of what they do."

He looked at her with a smile. "Exactly. It's not just a way to make money, but an art."

"Rather a twisted way to look at things," she said with a smile.

"There are more twisted things in this world than either of us can dream of," he said, the look on his face serious.

"Crazed things," she said with a sad look on her face. "This has been the vacation from hell. I can't believe we ended up in a little town in the bottom end of Texas."

"Tristan was the perfect place to hatch such a scheme. Small town surrounded by scrub brush and ranch land. The kind of place where the town's kids just want to escape. I've never seen such a down-and-out place. Ben had spent enough time there growing up that what he described to the buyer, the pictures, all of it was real. What wasn't real was the actual sale."

JUST BEFORE MIDNIGHT, Talib called. "How are you holding up?"

"Fine. It's Ava I'm worried about," he said.

"What I remember of Ava, she'll be fine. She's strong."

"What's up?"

"I have some news. The autopsy report on Kelsey Willows, the woman who took Ava's hospital bed," he clarified. "The report is back and strongly hinting at foul play. One of the cleaners saw a man he's confirmed is Ben Whyte from a picture enter the room just before her death. It's looking like murder."

"I suppose there'll be no resolution on that. Too bad."

"In a way," Talib said. "But Ben Whyte's dead and that can't be anything but a good thing."

"True," Faisal replied.

"This went all the way to the heart of Texas," Talib said. There was a hint of a smile in his voice. "There's other news, Faisal, and that's why I'm calling. They've identified the survivor I mentioned earlier. The Coast Guard just notified me. It's Dan Adams."

Minutes later, Faisal was giving the joyful news to Ava.

"Your father is alive," Faisal said. "He's weak but he's going to make it. He's en route to Miami now."

"Alive," Ava whispered. She could barely fathom the words. It was everything she had hoped for and nothing that she'd expected. "How?" She shook her head. "Never mind. It doesn't matter, what matters is that he's alive."

"And I heard he asked for you," Faisal said.

"He's conscious?"

"Amazingly, yes," Faisal said. "Your father's a survivor. I don't know anyone else who would have survived an attack and then over four days at sea. He was very lucky," he said seriously. "The yacht was reported by a container ship when it finally drifted into shipping lanes."

Ava reached for Faisal's hand, her palm grazing his. The heat of his skin on hers offered her the strength she needed. But still the questions remained. Her father was alive but was this nightmare truly over?

Mercy Hospital, Miami
Wednesday, June 15—2:00 p.m.

FAISAL STOOD BEHIND Ava in the doorway of the hospital room. Her father had been airlifted off the container ship that had found him. Faisal and Ava had left Tristan early this morning by helicopter.

They'd landed on a nearby private airstrip and he'd hired a driver to bring them here. He wouldn't leave her alone. It was too emotional for her. And that aside, he was invested too. This man was important to the family but, more important, he had to be here for Ava. The possibility that she might lose her father had been devastating for her. Now she hesitated in the doorway of his room as if she couldn't imagine after everything she had been through that this could be real.

He put an arm around her waist, giving her support even as he urged her forward. They slipped by the unsmiling security. Faisal's unconcealed handgun emphasized the seriousness of all that had transpired. Whether this was over or not, Faisal wasn't taking any chances.

"I can't believe it, I hoped…" She looked up at him with tears in her eyes.

"It's him, Ava. I promise you. He lived."

She leaned for a second against him. It was as if she were gathering strength. She reached up to gently run her fingers down his cheek before taking a step away from him.

The man had his back to them. He was emaciated

and his hair was grayer than Faisal remembered. Dan turned the wheelchair around. The distinctive features, the piercing brown eyes were exactly as he remembered.

"Dad!" Ava's voice was weak and seemed to break, even on that single-syllable word. But Faisal knew the word meant so much. She'd told him less than twenty-four hours ago that she thought she'd never be able to say it to him again. It had been her worst fear and her worst nightmare.

Faisal watched the two of them embrace and marveled at the fact that Dan Adams had lived. The yacht had drifted into the shipping lane and that appeared to be the only thing that had saved him. It had made him visible, or at least more visible for he'd still needed a passing ship to rescue him. But luck had held and somehow the yacht's trajectory had missed the worst of the hurricane. The Florida coast too had also missed the brunt of it. All in all, considering what had happened to get him in the situation, Dan Adams had been lucky. He'd survived the injuries that Ben Whyte had inflicted on him. In a nightmare of days and nights he'd still managed to survive.

For a minute there was silence as Ava hugged the man she'd called father for more than half of her life.

"I thought you were..." She couldn't say it. She choked on the word.

"Gone," he said with a half smile.

"Yes." She smiled, relieved at how things had

turned out. "I thought I'd never see you again. What happened? Are you alright?"

Dan looked at her sadly and Faisal stepped in to put a hand on Ava's shoulder as she knelt by her father. "Give your father some time."

"No," Dan said firmly as he looked at both of them. "I'm fine." He reached out, his arm bare and thin, the dark hair standing out against the pink and blistered skin.

"Why isn't this wrapped?" Ava said, her attention drawn to the arm as Faisal's had been.

"They're leaving it for now. Don't worry, honey." Dan's laugh was hardly a laugh at all but instead a dry sound that seemed to scrape from somewhere deep inside him. "I'll live and that's the main thing."

Ava made a small choking sound and wiped her eyes with the back of one hand. She stood and Faisal's arm went around her waist. She looked up at him.

"I'm okay," she reassured him.

"How did you ever get involved in anything so shady?" She looked at Faisal. It was a question that had remained unasked between them, for her father had always been a law-abiding upright man and to be involved with someone like Ben was incomprehensible. "An error in judgment?" she asked.

"It's over," Dan said with a weak smile. "Ben was a man who needed a helping hand, or so I thought. He took my intentions all wrong. That night on the yacht was desperation on his part." He shook his head. "It was my fault. Like a fool I told him that I couldn't go along with his scheme. It wasn't just men like Chan who were getting fleeced, he was taking hard-earned money from people who had little savings. Either way you looked at it, Chan or no Chan, rich or poor, it was criminal. But I should never have told him I was going to report him." He shook his head. "I can only say my anger got the best of me. It was an incredibly stupid move."

"How'd you find out what he was doing?" Ava asked.

"It was when Darrell Chan contacted me. It was clear then that something was up. He was the one that told me that he'd purchased land and had a deed with my signature on it completing the transfer. But it was his doubts about that second piece of land that had him contacting me in the first place and revealed this whole mess."

"Land was being sold by Ben Whyte that wasn't owned by him. Using your name on land you had no claim to or no knowledge of," Ava added. "Land he had no right to sell. Unbelievable."

"Forged deeds," Dan said. "I discovered that he was using my reputation to validate his scheme and selling tracts of land that he didn't own, and forged my signature on two transfers. It was at that point that I knew that I had to do something. But I still thought that I could talk sense into Ben." He shook his head.

"You set up a meeting with me to have it investigated," Faisal said.

"Exactly. I wanted to make sure my suspicions

were right. I'd always planned to notify the authorities," her father said softly. "I just waited too long to do it."

"Ben took out the navigation and computer system. There was no way to track you," Faisal said. "How did you survive getting shot and then knocked overboard?"

"I was lucky enough to grab a rope on the way down. Although I still ended up treading water for a bit. And Ava—" he looked at her with a slow smile "—had left her window open. I finally managed to crawl in there. I found her phone and called for help, but I wasn't connected long enough to trace." He shrugged. "I suppose it wouldn't have mattered anyway, the yacht was drifting. I can't tell you what happened immediately after that. It was the last thing I remembered for hours. When I came to, I crawled to the upper deck. Literally crawled," he said as his hand brushed against the bandages on his thigh and he glanced at his right leg, which was in a cast. "And again that was the last thing I remember for a long while. I was in and out after that. I was just lucky they found me when they did."

"Oh, Dad." Ava put her arms around him. "We were both lucky. I don't know what I would have done if I'd lost you."

She let him go and took a step back.

"But there's more?"

"I'm afraid there is." He shook his head. "What happened is my fault."

"Dad, no…"

"Ava, listen," he said. "I shouldn't have gotten involved. I should have called the authorities immediately," he said. "I'll regret that until the day I die. I made a mistake," Dan said. "You could have died."

"I didn't," Ava said. "You're an honorable man."

"A stupid one who should have played along, at least I should never have…"

"It's okay, Dad," Ava said. "We all lived through it."

Dan was quiet for a minute. "I'll be going home after all this." He looked at Ava as if waiting for her to join in. "How about a short vacation before you start…"

"My new job," Ava finished as she shook her head, taking both her stepfather's hands in hers. "I can't, Dad. No more delays. I know you'll be okay and I'll visit at Christmas, I promise. But for now, I need to get my own life going in Wyoming." She looked back at Faisal.

"I see," Dan said softly.

"Dad…"

"No, sweetheart, I really do." He looked at Faisal and a silent understanding seemed to pass between the two men. "I'm tired. Maybe you two could come back later to visit." He looked back as a nurse entered the room. "Besides, I won't be here that much longer. My doctor said they had plans to discharge me."

"That's right," the nurse said with a smile as she overheard the last part. "I heard you'll be discharged in a few days."

"It can't happen soon enough," Dan said with a smile as he looked at the arm Faisal had around his daughter's waist.

Chapter Twenty-Six

Friday, June 17

"I hate to leave him," Ava said.

It was two days since they'd found her father and he was well on the way to recovery. She'd spent time at her father's bedside but she'd also spent time with Faisal. He'd offered her a suite in the luxury hotel his family owned and that he called his home away from home. But she'd spent more time with him than in the suite he offered, as they made up for the time they had lost. They'd laughed together and they'd seen a different side of Miami, a more laid-back, romantic side, as they strolled the beach at sunset and had supper in a quaint café they discovered by accident one day. Now, the late afternoon sun streamed in through the picture window as she sank into the thick luxuriousness of a mint-green leather couch. When they'd left her father after learning he'd been found, she'd felt at peace for the first time in days, knowing that he was safe. Now, she glanced around the Nassar company–

owned penthouse suite in Miami. It was luxury with
a toned-down touch. Classic rock played in the background and reminded her of Faisal's love for seventies-
era rock. Five years ago, she'd shared that love with
him at parties and even a few lazy evenings like this.
But she'd been twenty then. It seemed a long time ago.
She held a cup of tea, a soft blanket over her shoulders
as she tucked one foot beneath her and stretched the
other leg out. "Dad's been through a lot and when he's
discharged he'll be going home alone…" Her voice
trailed off and her lips tightened. "I don't like it, but…"

"You can't be late to start your own life." He cupped
her chin, his eyes looking into hers. "You have a career to begin, a life ahead of you, a new job waiting.
Your father knows that."

"I know." She smiled as he dropped his hand and
put his arm around her shoulders. "I can't wait for that,
at least I couldn't until all of this."

"It will be fine. The excitement for your career will
come back. The memory of this trauma will fade."

"Will it?"

"I promise," he said with a low growl in his voice.

"Still, I owe him—"

"You owe it to him to be happy," Faisal said, looking at her with a smile. "You heard what the doctor
said, he'll be discharged soon," Faisal assured her as
they sat in the Miami penthouse suite. The suite belonged to the Al-Nassar family but was used primar-
ily by him. "You need to start your own life, your own

career," he repeated as if saying the words in a different way would somehow make them more real to her.

"How did you get so smart? You're right. That's exactly what my father would want." She lowered her teacup and looked at him with a sheen of tears in her eyes. It was all so much to comprehend and yet she still felt she owed her father.

"He wants nothing but your happiness," he said.

"I know you're right. He's said it often enough to me."

"It's what every parent wants. I know mine did and I know Dan does too," he said.

She looked at him and saw something else in his eyes, a hint of nostalgia, sadness even. She put the tea down and took both his hands in hers. "I'm so sorry, Faisal. You lost your parents when you were a teenager. And here I am thinking of going off, of leaving him—"

"Ava, quit dramatizing," Faisal interrupted with a smile. "My parents' accident was tragic but it has nothing to do with any of this. Sure, I'd change it if I could, but even so, no parent would hold back their child. That's what kids do, grow up."

She looked down at her hands and smiled at the fact that they looked so small, almost lost in his. He seemed to notice not at all. Instead he pulled her against his chest, his arm going around her as if he was never going to let her go.

"I think it's time we began thinking about our own lives, our own family."

"What do you mean 'our'?" She looked at him with a frown, her beautiful eyes troubled.

"Don't deny that there's something special between us. There always has been."

She met that statement with silence.

"I know we were apart…"

"Five years," she said with a hint of regret. "I thought of you often."

"I love you, Ava. I always have. And now with you in the same state, there isn't even geography to separate us."

"That never separated us," she whispered.

"No, you're right. It was our youth."

She turned her face up, an invitation she'd wanted to offer a long time ago. He took it as easily as she'd dreamed in the past. He leaned down and kissed her with all the passion of the unsaid words that lay between them.

"Come with me," he said thickly. He led her to a bedroom hidden down a hallway of soaring ceilings and skylights. The skylights dusted sunshine along the mellow wood floor. The floor reminded her that he had told her all those years ago that he was restoring old flooring he'd obtained from a demolished church. The old and the new wove together to make the suite breathtaking. On the floor by the sprawling bed was a woven Moroccan wool rug, its colors a dark, muted brown that was accentuated with patches of cream. Overhead a skylight streamed light into the room. Against one wall was a stereo system with a collection of vintage vinyl records lined up on either side. She didn't see any more after that. Instead, she let him lead her to the downy seduction of the bed, which seemed to fill the room with a promise.

It was she who pulled him down onto the bed as she fell backward, playfully testing whether it was as soft and as inviting as it looked. But it was his firm lips on hers, his readiness against her that took all her playfulness to the next level. Their clothes disappeared in their roughhousing of play and desire. An hour later they lay naked in each other's arms.

"This is how it was meant to be," she whispered. "I hear Wyoming calling."

"Just Wyoming?" Faisal said with a laugh.

"For the moment, yes," she said with an answering laugh. "I love you, do you know that?"

"I should hope so," Faisal said. "I don't want to lose you again. I only hope you feel the same way."

"You won't be given that option," she said with a smile in her voice.

He leaned over and kissed her, hard and deep, and yet briefly. When he rose up on an elbow, he looked into her eyes. "You're everything to me, do you know that, Ava? I love you," he finished before she could reply.

Tears glistened in her eyes as she reached up to draw him to her. "I wish every moment of our life could be like this," she said.

"Like what?" he asked thickly.

"Spent together."

He ran a thumb along her collarbone. "That sounds perfect to me. Any way we cut it, we'll be together…"

"Forever," she finished. "It's everything I want, Faisal."

"We'll be married," he said as he plopped down beside her.

"What kind of marriage proposal is that?" she asked with a giggle. She turned over on one elbow so they were nose to nose. Chest to breast, and despite how erotic it all was, for a moment they were serious.

"Ava Adams, would you do me the honor of being my wife?"

"Forever and always," she replied as her lips met his. And the kiss seemed to last forever.

When the kiss finally ended, they lay shoulder to shoulder. The air-conditioning caressed their heated skin and Ava thought she might have reached nirvana. It was then that Faisal reached under the pillow and brought out a box. "To seal the deal, my love."

"Are you always going to be this romantic?" she said with what she knew was a loving, yet sarcastic edge to her voice.

"Open it," he said with only a small hint of the Al-Nassar command she'd teased him about when they'd been together at school.

She opened the box and saw a ring that was like none she'd seen before nestled in a satin bed. She wouldn't even ask how he'd gotten it so quickly. She was quickly learning that it was the Al-Nassar way. Instead, she could only look at it with damp eyes. The band was delicate strands of gold that appeared to be braided together. The heart-shaped diamond sparkled in its setting. The ring truly reflected the love he'd so recently admitted.

"It's beautiful." The words weren't enough and yet that was all she could say. "It's unique, romantic…" Tears threatened. She had no words to explain how she felt. It was a moment she'd never dreamed of despite how she'd always felt about Faisal. He'd been everything. He was everything.

"You're everything," she said as if he would know what she meant.

And the look in his eyes told her that she had said it all.

"It represents my love and the love of family."

"You mean children?" she asked, looking into his dark eyes.

"Maybe or maybe just the love of those we allow into our lives."

"That's beautiful, Fai," she said, leaning over to kiss him.

He pulled her closer. His eyes looked deeply into hers. Then he kissed her, long and hard and hot. The kiss lasted a minute and then two before it ended. She looked at him with all the love she was feeling, the ring clutched in the palm of her fisted right hand as if she would never let it go.

But a few minutes later she watched as he slipped the ring onto her finger. A ring that was unique and rare, much like the man she'd always admired and loved and had now agreed to marry. It was a ring fashioned from love, hope and a promise.

Outside the sun shone even brighter as it offered all the hope and warmth of the promise of their future together.

* * * * *

Check out the previous books in the
DESERT JUSTICE *series:*

SHEIK'S RESCUE
SHEIK'S RULE
SON OF THE SHEIK

Available now from Harlequin Intrigue!

YOU CAN FIND MORE INFORMATION ON UPCOMING HARLEQUIN® TITLES, FREE EXCERPTS AND MORE AT WWW.HARLEQUIN.COM.

HICNM0717

"I want to ask you about your babies," Nikki said. "Oakley and
Jesse Rose?" Was it her imagination or did the woman clutch
the dolls even harder to her thin chest?

"What happened the night they disappeared?" Did Nikki
really expect an answer? She could hope, couldn't she? Mostly,
she needed to hear the sound of her voice in this claustrophobic
room. The rocking had a hypnotic effect, like being pulled
down a rabbit hole.

"Everyone outside this room believes you had something to
do with it. You and Nate Corwin." No response, no reaction to
the name. "Was he your lover?"

She moved closer, catching the decaying scent that rose from
the rocking chair as if the woman was already dead. "I don't
believe it's true. But I think you might know who kidnapped
your babies," she whispered.

The speculation at the time was that the kidnapping had been
an inside job. Marianne had been suffering from postpartum
depression. The nanny had said that Mrs. McGraw was having
trouble bonding with the babies and that she'd been afraid to
leave Marianne alone with them.

And, of course, there'd been Marianne's secret lover—the man everyone believed had helped her kidnap her own children. He'd been implicated because of a shovel found in the stables with his bloody fingerprints on it—along with fresh soil—even though no fresh graves had been found.

"Was Nate Corwin involved, Marianne?" The court had decided that Marianne McGraw couldn't have acted alone. To get both babies out the second-story window, she would have needed an accomplice.

"Did my father help you?"

There was no sign that the woman even heard her, let alone recognized her alleged lover's name. And if the woman had answered, Nikki knew she would have jumped out of her skin.

She checked to make sure Tess wasn't watching as she snapped a photo of the woman in the rocker. The flash lit the room for an instant and made a snap sound. As she started to take another, she thought she heard a low growling sound coming from the rocker.

She hurriedly took another photo, though hesitantly, as the growling sound seemed to grow louder. Her eye on the viewfinder, she was still focused on the woman in the rocker when Marianne McGraw seemed to rock forward as if lurching from her chair.

A shriek escaped her before she could pull down the camera. She had closed her eyes and thrown herself back, slamming into the wall. Pain raced up one shoulder. She stifled a scream as she waited for the feel of the woman's clawlike fingers on her throat.

But Marianne McGraw hadn't moved. It had only been a trick of the light. And yet, Nikki noticed something different about the woman.

Marianne was smiling.

Don't miss
DARK HORSE by B.J. Daniels,
available August 2017 wherever
Harlequin® Intrigue books and ebooks are sold.

www.Harlequin.com

HIEXP0717

Earn points from all your Harlequin book purchases from wherever you shop.

Turn your points into *FREE BOOKS* of your choice
OR
EXCLUSIVE GIFTS from your favorite authors or series.

Join for FREE today at
www.HarlequinMyRewards.com.

Harlequin My Rewards is a free program (no fees) without any commitments or obligations.

MYR17

LOVE
Harlequin
romance?

Join our Harlequin community to share your thoughts and connect with other romance readers!

Be the first to find out about promotions, news, and exclusive content!

Sign up for the Harlequin e-newsletter and download a free book from any series at

www.TryHarlequin.com

CONNECT WITH US AT:

Harlequin.com/Community

 Facebook.com/HarlequinBooks

Twitter.com/HarlequinBooks

Instagram.com/HarlequinBooks

Pinterest.com/HarlequinBooks

ReaderService.com

H HARLEQUIN®

**ROMANCE WHEN
YOU NEED IT**

THE WORLD IS BETTER WITH

Romance

Harlequin has everything from contemporary, passionate and heartwarming to suspenseful and inspirational stories.

Whatever your mood,
we have a romance just for you!

Connect with us to find your next great read,
special offers and more.

f /HarlequinBooks

y @HarlequinBooks

www.HarlequinBlog.com

www.Harlequin.com/Newsletters